TEAROOM
mysteries

Dear Reader,

Have you ever felt like the world was trying to give you a sign? This book is about searching for meaning in signs that don't always seem to make sense: everything from secret codes in newspapers to the stars the Wise Men followed to find the baby Jesus at Christmastime, when this story takes place.

Jan thinks she's found a code hidden in the local paper, and is all too eager to decode it. In the same newspaper stories, Elaine thinks she may be seeing intimate details of her life as a girl, although she doesn't want to believe it.

But this story is about other signs as well: signs of Christmas in the decorations that festoon both the tearoom and the town, and even more importantly in the holiday cheer that fills the streets. And signs of change, as Jan prepares for her wedding and Elaine considers her own future.

As you read, I hope it will help you consider the signs in your own life. Good things and big realizations don't always arrive all at once. Sometimes it takes time to understand what's right in front of us, and sometimes it takes work to uncover the clues that lead us to the truth. But whatever you're facing or wondering about, I hope this book will help you pay attention to the little signs and wonders that crowd each of our lives each day—and follow them wherever they may lead.

Vera Dodge

Tearoom Mysteries

Tearoom for Two
Tea Rose
To a Tea
Crosswords and Chamomile
Burning Secrets
O Christmas Tea
On Thin Ice
Tea Is for Treasure
Trouble Brewing
Mystery and Macarons
The Tea Will Tell
Tea and Touchdowns
Steeped in Secrets
Stealing Santa
A Monumental Mystery
Whispers from the Past
Tearoom in a Tempest
Brimming with Questions
Beneath the Surface
Apart at the Seams
Turning the Tables
In Too Deep
Do You See What I See?

Do You See What I See?

VERA DODGE

Guideposts
New York

Tearoom Mysteries is a trademark of Guideposts

Published by Guideposts Books & Inspirational Media
110 William Street
New York, New York 10038
Guideposts.org

Acknowledgments

Every attempt has been made to credit the sources of copyrighted material used in this book. If any such acknowledgment has been inadvertently omitted or miscredited, receipt of such information would be appreciated.

Cover and interior design by Müllerhaus
Cover illustration by Ross Jones, represented by Deborah Wolfe, Ltd.
Typeset by Aptara, Inc.

Printed and bound in the United States of America
10 9 8 7 6 5 4 3 2 1

CHAPTER ONE

Elaine!" Jan Blake called as the front door of the tearoom *thunked* shut behind her. "Elaine!"

Elaine Cook had been running up a column of numbers in her office and feeling pleasantly satisfied to see that their business was in a healthy state, even before the rush of Christmas parties and out-of-town shoppers they expected to come through the door of the tearoom in the coming days.

But at the sound of alarm in Jan's voice, Elaine dropped the pencil on the sheet of numbers on the desk and rushed out into the entryway to meet her cousin.

Jan's cheeks were bright pink from the cold outside. Her dark hair, with a hint of gray in it, was normally patted into place with the same care Jan took over everything, but now it had blown away from her face in her rush to come in from outdoors and was sticking out in all kinds of directions. Jan's blue eyes were bright with urgency. "I'm so glad you're here," she said. Jan's hands were red from the bitter weather and filled with scraps of what appeared to be lace.

"Where have you been?" Elaine asked, trying to remember if Jan had mentioned where she was headed when she left the house that morning. "What happened?"

By now Rose Young, their employee who had been serving a pair of customers in the east parlor, joined them.

"Is everything all right?" Rose asked in a low tone as the customers glanced at them curiously.

"I don't know," Jan said, shaking her head.

From the west parlor, their second employee, Archie Bentham, hurried to Jan's side. His shock of silver hair, which veered closer and closer to true white each season, belied his energetic nature.

Archie had been polishing one of their silver tea sets to a high shine that would probably be fit for the Queen of England herself, and still held the soft rag, covered with tarnish, in his hand. "Jan," he said, with his delightfully plummy British accent, "what is the matter?"

Elaine had hoped that the customers would be distracted from their little gathering by the excellent quality of the tearoom's tea, the deliciousness of Jan's scones, or the beautiful Christmas decorations they'd spent an entire day putting up just after Thanksgiving. They'd wrapped the hall banister in juniper swag, filled the tables with holly and carnation flower arrangements and glowing red candles, and topped all of it with a healthy dose of period-appropriate lace and sparkling reproductions of Victorian angel ornaments, who played harps, sang songs, and looked heavenward from just about any place you could see in the tearoom.

But apparently the entire staff of the tearoom congregating by the door was more interesting than even Jan's most recent Christmas-themed creation—cranberry scones with cinnamon glaze. The whole population of the east parlor had turned their heads now to see what was going on.

"Let's talk about it in the kitchen," Elaine said.

As Elaine hustled Jan toward the back of the sprawling Victorian home that housed the tearoom, Archie Bentham addressed the crowd of curious customers. "May I get any of you anything? More tea? A bit of clotted cream?"

Just as it always did, Archie's accent seemed to work on the gathered clientele like magic. All around the parlor, Elaine could see smiles emerge and heads shake as their customers remembered that Rose had taken perfect care of each of them and there wasn't a single thing any of them needed.

Back in the kitchen, Elaine settled Jan onto the tall stool which was one of Jan's favorite perches when she sat at the counter working out the details of some new recipe, or making her own signature changes to an old favorite.

Archie and Rose lined up on either side of Elaine, still concerned, but ready to do whatever it took, just as soon as they understood what was going on.

"Now," Elaine said, "where were you?"

Jan looked surprised to discover that Elaine didn't already know, which happened to the cousins every now and then. Because they lived and worked so closely together, it was easy to forget that everything one knew didn't automatically transmit to the other, just by osmosis.

"I was at Bob's," she said.

At the mention of her new fiancé's name, a huge smile spread across Jan's face—the same smile that had given Elaine the hint a few years ago that Bob Claybrook might one day become Jan's second husband.

For an instant, Elaine thought of the home Bob had occupied when he and Jan first started dating. But then she corrected herself. Bob was just across the street now, in the house he had bought so that he and Jan could stay close to the tearoom—and Elaine—even after Jan and Bob were married.

Elaine was grateful for Bob's thoughtfulness on her account, and for Jan's. She would never have stood in the way of her cousin's happiness, but when she and Jan had opened the tearoom, both of them had thought they would spend their old age together. It touched her that Jan and Bob hadn't wanted to leave her out, even as they moved into what she hoped would be a beautiful new chapter of their own lives.

"Is everything all right?" Elaine asked carefully. "With Bob?"

Jan looked up, seemingly surprised. "Of course," she said. Then worry formed in her eyes. "Why? Do you know something? Is he all right?"

"No, no," Elaine said. "As far as I know he's fine."

Jan sighed with relief. Then her brow furrowed. "But he doesn't know what to do either," she said.

"About what?" Elaine asked, trying to hide both her worry and her impatience.

Behind her, Archie crossed his arms in preparation, as if girding himself to go out and give a good thumping to anyone who might have made the mistake of messing with either of his employers.

Jan threw the fistful of lace scraps she had been holding down on the counter. “This lace!” she said, sounding exasperated.

Elaine’s eyes widened in surprise before she managed to compose her face into what she hoped was a sympathetic expression.

In the last week or so, as Jan finally turned her attention to planning the upcoming wedding, she had become awash in plans, all of which were both urgent and impracticable. Elaine didn’t know what to make of it. She’d been to Jan’s first wedding, to Peter, and even when Jan was a much younger blushing bride, she hadn’t made such a big production of the ceremony. That one had been simple and sensible, just like Jan: a satin dress her mother had made, a bouquet of blue flowers picked from the backyard, and lemonade and cake in the church basement. In Elaine’s mind, that was pretty much the perfect wedding. But, of course, she knew better than to say that.

“What about the lace?” Elaine asked gently.

Jan looked up at her as if trying to restrain her impatience that the problem wasn’t as glaringly obvious to Elaine as it was to her.

“Which one?” she asked simply. “I found these pieces of lace in one of mom’s old boxes,” Jan said. “I’m pretty sure I remember her saying they belonged to my great-grandmother. I thought I could use them to wrap the bridesmaids’ bouquets.”

At her first wedding, Jan had only had one attendant. But this time she decided to have four bridesmaids. Elaine was more than honored to stand up for her cousin, but she had been surprised at Jan's choice to have a gaggle of bridesmaids.

"That sounds lovely," Elaine said as Jan spread the pieces on the counter.

"But look," Jan sighed. Several of the pieces of lace were only about the size of a saucer, not big enough to wrap any substantial bouquet. One seemed to have been a table runner, a yard or so long. "Most of them are too small. And this one is too long," she said.

As Jan spoke, Archie began to quietly back away from the group, apparently having assured himself that no real emergency was, in fact, afoot. On Elaine's other side, Rose unobtrusively faded back to pick up a pot of hot water and some tea balls, then slipped out of the kitchen, returning to the customers in the parlor.

Elaine knit her eyebrows. She knew better than to tell Jan that it didn't actually matter that much. Telling a bride, at any age, that the details of her wedding weren't of crucial importance to the rest of the world was a sure way to bring on a storm of unpleasant emotions.

"What did Bob say?" Elaine asked. Bob was always sensible, and there was a good chance he had made some reasonable suggestion. If so, maybe she could encourage Jan in that direction and solve the "emergency" to everyone's satisfaction.

"He thought I should cut this one up!" Jan said. She pointed to the table runner and gave Elaine a stricken look, as if Bob had suggested cutting up a first edition copy of the King James Bible.

Elaine took a deep breath. Bob's good sense had failed to mend the situation this time, although she could hardly blame him. In his position, it must have sounded like a reasonable solution. But now she'd have to depend on her own wits. "Well," she said, "you already wanted to use that Italian ribbon you found to wrap the stems of the bouquets, right?"

Jan nodded. "That's right," she said.

"If you wrap the stems in lace," Elaine said, "you wouldn't be able to see the ribbon. What if you did it the other way around? Wrap the stems in ribbon and attach a flash of lace as part of the bouquet?"

"Part of the bouquet?" Jan repeated.

"Sure," Elaine said. "Just like another flower."

"That might be beautiful," Jan said, her eyes lighting up.

"I think it would be," said Elaine. She tapped on each of the small pieces of lace. "Three, four, five," she counted. "That's enough for all four bridesmaids. Me, Rose, Tara, and Paula." Amy, Jan's daughter, had decided to support the couple from the front row; she would be far along in her pregnancy, or may even have had her baby at that point. "And a piece for your own bouquet, if you want it."

As Jan's eyes drifted to the long rectangle of lace still lying on the counter, Elaine quickly composed a role for it. "We can set that runner out at the wedding tea," she said. "It's too big to carry in the ceremony, but it can still be part of the day."

At the mention of the wedding tea, all the hopeful light that had begun to build in Jan's eyes drained away.

"The wedding tea," she repeated, as if she were pronouncing the syllables of the name of a mortal enemy.

Elaine laid a comforting hand on her cousin's shoulder. When she first heard Jan mention the wedding tea, it had sounded like a great idea. Instead of a rehearsal dinner, Jan had said, she wanted to have a wedding tea. They'd do it before the rehearsal, rather than after, so that everyone involved in the wedding could get to know one another. And then they'd head home right after the rehearsal the night before the wedding, which would give all of them a chance to get some really good rest before the morning.

What could be simpler? Elaine had thought. They already had everything they needed to throw a world-class tea, and they'd been practicing hosting people at Tea for Two together for almost three years. But as the planning had progressed, it now seemed like a lot of things might be simpler than putting on the wedding tea of Jan's visions.

For one thing, it was going to be a very big crowd. But most important, the idea was for Elaine and Jan both to be able to feel like guests at the event, not servers. And since Archie and Rose were also like family to the cousins, they wanted them to be able to be guests, not servers, as well. That presented a problem as to who would organize and direct hired caterers during the event. So they'd started to try to think about other venues, but hadn't settled on anything yet.

Elaine had spent the last several days picking away at these problems with Jan. She knew they were no closer to a solution now than they had been the last time they talked about it. And she knew talking about it any further right now would only make things worse.

Lord, she prayed, *we can't see the way here. Will you help us?*

As she finished, her glance fell on a copy of the paper, left out on the counter beside the lace.

"Is that the latest *Courier*?" Elaine asked, her eyes lighting up with delight.

"I guess so," Jan said.

"We haven't read the new installment of *The Crooked Lake Mystery*," Elaine said.

At this, Jan perked up. The *Penzance Courier* had been running an unusual feature for the past several weeks, a serialized mystery novel set in a small town very much like Lancaster.

"It's the second to the last," Jan said. "Maybe we can guess who did it by now."

Elaine grinned, picking up the paper. "Maybe you'll find another clue with your crazy codeword search."

"It's not crazy," Jan said. "Last week there was a clear message."

Elaine shook her head tolerantly. Captivated by an early installment of the story, Jan had noticed that first letter of each word down the left side of the column spelled out another word: *please*. Then, in later installments, she thought she'd found others. Elaine suspected it was all just coincidence. Look down the columns of any paper and some of them must make a word every now and then. But she wasn't about to contradict Jan now that she'd finally gotten her off the topic of the wedding.

"We're going to have to flip a coin to figure out who gets to read it first," Elaine said. But as she spoke, she had an idea. "Or...," she said.

"Or what?" Jan asked.

"You know what?" Elaine said. "I think we could both use a break. Why don't we curl up in a corner in the sitting room and I'll read it to you?"

"That sounds wonderful," Jan said with relief. "Let me just get us a cup of tea."

For the next hour or so, the two of them sat together upstairs, Jan rapt while Elaine read the new chapter of the mystery. The setting was so familiar that it actually made Elaine a little bit uneasy, wondering if their little town could hide all the secrets that the characters in the fictional town were dealing with.

And she wasn't the only one who felt that way.

"It's so strange," Jan said at one point, when one of the characters drove up in a white hard-top convertible with candy-apple red finish. "I remember Jim Biggers had a car just like that when we were in high school."

Elaine smiled. She had dated Jim briefly and always thought of him with fondness. But the similarities between this story and the pleasant drives she remembered with Jim ended with the superficial details of the car.

This story was actually quite dark, about betrayal, frustrated dreams, broken hearts...and possibly murder.

"If it's in the *Courier,*" Elaine said lightly, "it's probably by a local author. That car of Jim's was famous. I'm sure we're not the only ones who remember it. It was probably just an easy detail for the author to sneak in."

"Keep reading," Jan said impatiently. "And then what happened?"

So Elaine went on, reading the story until it ended on a cliffhanger, with the heroine of the story calling and calling the hero, but getting no answer.

CHAPTER TWO

Elaine had been hoping for a quiet moment to herself to grab a cup of coffee and think over her day, but when she walked into the kitchen the next morning, it looked as though a bomb filled with scones had gone off.

Or perhaps not quite like a bomb. The dozens and dozens of scones scattered around the room weren't thrown around helter-skelter as a bomb blast would have rendered them. Instead, they were neatly stacked on cooling racks on pretty much every surface in the place: all the counters, of course, but also stacked on Elaine's papers, tucked away in the toaster nook, perched on the top of the refrigerator.

"Which of these do you like best?" Jan asked, holding out a pair of scones, which had both been baked to a flaky, golden perfection.

Beside her, Jan's granddaughter Avery stood, off school for Christmas break, and looking at Elaine with sober eyes, her own hands and apron covered with dough, just like her grandmother's.

Elaine opened her mouth, prepared as always to give an honest answer, but for the life of her, she couldn't see a difference between them.

"They both look wonderful," Elaine said.

Jan and Avery each gazed at Elaine with an air of disappointment, as if she had just revealed she didn't think there was much difference between a diamond ring and one made out of glass.

"One of them has *a whole tablespoon* more butter," Avery informed Elaine, still with a tone of shock that her cousin wouldn't be able to recognize a difference so profound.

There were so many scones crowding the room that Elaine hadn't even noticed Rose, who she now saw was doing her best to prepare for the day, prefilling ramekins of clotted cream and thick local preserves to be served with each order of scones. But because Jan's project had taken up so much of the counter space, she was doing her best to fill the dozens of small ceramic cups on a tiny lip of counter that remained just beside the sink, where she had stashed the jars of jam and cream. It didn't look as though Jan had stopped to do a single dish since whenever her baking extravaganza had begun, likely in the wee hours of that morning.

When Rose glanced up, Elaine gave her a sympathetic look, but Rose answered with a smile. As with so many things, Rose was taking this all in stride.

"What about these?" Jan asked.

Elaine turned back to her cousin. Avery was holding out a scone that had been painstakingly hand-frosted with a series of delicate X-marks that came together in the shape of a lacy pink-frosting heart.

"That's beautiful," Elaine said, glad she was able to give a compliment that was both spontaneous and heartfelt. "It looks like your grandmother's cross-stitch."

Avery beamed under the praise, but as Elaine looked at the horde of scones that surrounded Jan, her heart sank. Jan must have decorated at least a few dozen scones with the same design. How long had it taken her? And who in the world was going to eat all these scones? There were enough for an entire week's worth of customers.

"That was the idea," Jan said. "But now I wonder if it's too much."

Elaine looked around the kitchen, marveling over the fact that Jan had managed to ask herself that question about the frosting, but not about the sheer number of scones in the place.

As she did, she caught sight of Archie Bentham swinging through the kitchen door, his mouth open to give an airy greeting.

But before he did, he took one look at the state of the kitchen, quickly closed his mouth, raised his eyebrows at Elaine, and backed right out.

"You know what?" Elaine said. "I think everyone will love whatever you choose."

Jan shook her head in dissatisfaction. "Everyone always says they love what I make," she said. "But it's not every day I get married."

"These are…for the wedding tea?" Elaine asked, wondering how they could possibly preserve them that long.

"Avery and I are just trying some ideas out," Jan said. "It's a dry run. Once I make up my mind, then I'll just whip up a few batches that day."

Elaine took a deep breath, resolving to wait for another time to suggest that Jan might have more important things on her plate the day before her wedding than making dozens of scones.

"Well," she said, "I can't make scones like you do, but can I at least help you clean up?"

"Oh, no!" Jan said with surprise. "We're not done."

"We still have to try the peach rosemary recipe," Avery said.

Jan nodded. "We'll just be a little while yet. Don't mind us."

At this, Elaine could see Rose's shoulders slump slightly beside the sink.

"Rose," Elaine said, "could you help me in the west parlor?"

Rose followed her out of the room. "Thank you. I didn't know what to do," Rose said. "I've been trying to stay out of her way, but there's not even room in there to get ready for the day."

"Not to fear," Archie said, joining them. "I can set up a tea station on one of these buffets. We can serve from here, instead of the kitchen. It will actually be quite English of us. The upper crust love to show off the talents of their staff. Why hide us back in the kitchen when you can have the pleasure of seeing us work in person?"

Elaine thought it over. "I love that, but I also don't want our customers to feel like we're breathing down their necks," she said.

"Not to worry!" Archie assured her. "If the English know anything, it's how to stay unobtrusive."

"And I'll make sure that if they do notice us, everyone feels comfortable," Rose said.

"All right, you two," Elaine said. "That sounds like a good plan to me. Just bring out everything you can, and we'll stage it from the west parlor instead of the kitchen."

"Aye, aye," said Archie, who also had a penchant for pretending that Jan and Elaine were the captains of a large, tea-dispensing ship.

"And I'll just...," Elaine said, looking around the room as Archie and Rose disappeared back into the kitchen for provisions. "I guess I'll just go out for a while."

"Elaine!" someone called from the east parlor, just as Elaine headed out the door.

When Elaine turned around, she saw Priscilla Gates, the librarian, waving at her. Elaine walked over to the table by the window where Priscilla was seated.

"Merry Christmas!" Priscilla said. She looked down at the plate before her, which held not one, but two scones: a sweet chocolate and cherry and a savory ham with chive. At the rate Priscilla was consuming scones, Elaine reflected, they might actually be able to find a home for all the ones Jan currently had stashed in the back. Or maybe Priscilla's obvious love for scones was part of what had cemented her friendship with Jan.

"Merry Christmas," Elaine said. She glanced at a bag at Priscilla's feet. "Been shopping?"

Priscilla nodded happily. "Got all my Christmas presents," she said. "At the bookstore," she added with a wink. "And I have to confess, there may be one or two treats in that bag for me."

"I'm curious about what books are good enough that a librarian would buy them," Elaine said.

"That'd be a good list!" Priscilla said. "I should make it up—and then post it in the library, to let people know they can take them out."

Elaine laughed.

"Say," Priscilla said, "is Jan in the back? I'd love to pop my head in and see her, but I didn't want to presume."

Elaine pursed her lips, thinking of the scene in the kitchen. "She is," she said, "but I think now may not be the best time."

"That's why I asked!" Priscilla said. "Well, please give her my best."

"Of course," Elaine said. "Enjoy your scones. And don't be shy—there are plenty more where that came from."

"I was afraid you were going to say that," Priscilla said with a wink.

A few minutes later, Elaine walked down the steps of the beloved old Tea for Two Victorian, purse slung over her shoulder.

But before she walked away, she turned to get one more glimpse of the big old house, as she always tried to do when she left the house around Christmastime. She loved seeing it decorated for Christmas, and there weren't too many more days left when she'd get to see the sight of the place decked with greenery that was threaded with thick red velvet ribbon, the twinkle lights hidden inside glowing, even in daylight, and the simple stalks of white candles visible in every one of their front windows.

The town, as she walked into the downtown area, was glittering with Christmas cheer. The streets already boasted the perfect old glass streetlights, but every single one was now wound with evergreen rope, dotted with white lights and glittering silver ornaments. Swags of pine branches hung over the street, between the buildings, creating something close to a canopy of evergreen. The shop windows were filled with holiday glitter: snowscapes filled with cotton snow, brightly colored packages that allowed passersby to guess endlessly at what wonderful mysteries must lie within, red plaid shirts, and sleds decorated with red ribbons. And one of the churches in town that year had set up a new fund-raising event, with high school kids selling roasted chestnuts on a downtown corner.

"Do you think it's a teddy bear or a new sweater?" a familiar voice asked Elaine as she stopped to look at a stack of presents piled in the window of the hardware store.

"Pastor Mike!" Elaine said, turning around with a smile. Then she looked back at the boxes. "I was always hoping for a pony myself."

"It'd have to be a small pony to fit in that box," the pastor said with a grin.

"That would be perfect," Elaine said. "He can keep Earl Grey company in the yard. And maybe cut down on how often we have to mow the grass."

"Always thinking, always thinking," the pastor said, tapping his temple. "That's what I like about you, Elaine."

"You on your way to the church?" she asked.

"Not yet," Pastor Mike said, shaking his head. "I'm looking for something for my wife. I always start out with the best intentions, but somehow I always find myself still looking a few days before Christmas."

"I'm sure you'll find something wonderful," Elaine said. "I mean, here in Lancaster—how could you not?"

"Maybe this is why I always leave it to the last minute," the pastor said, nodding to her as he walked on.

It was still early for lunch, Elaine thought, but maybe that meant there was time to call Nathan Culver, her boyfriend, and confirm their dinner tonight. In the past few weeks, things hadn't felt quite right between them. Maybe it had just been all the excitement of trying to find Jan's granddaughter Avery, who'd gotten lost in the wilderness a few weeks ago on a camping trip, but Elaine was beginning to have doubts about that.

As she crunched down the snowy street, catching glimpses of Chickadee Lake each time she passed between houses or stores, she wondered if it might be something else. It wasn't just that she and Nathan hadn't spent much time together lately, which was understandable. The fall and winter were a busy time for auctions, and as one of the most respected auctioneers in the county, or perhaps even in the state, Nathan was in high demand. When she had last seen Nathan, she had felt a distance between them, as if he was interested in just about everything in the world but her. Or as if he had something so big on his mind that he couldn't really think about anything else.

In that case, though, wouldn't he share it with her? The thought gave her comfort, and pause. Nathan was usually so naturally open and honest. He'd been the first to declare his feelings for her, after all. And if he was brave enough to do that, not knowing how she felt in return, what else would he hide from her?

Maybe, Elaine thought, it was all in her head. In fact, maybe she was the one who had been acting strange. She had certainly felt strange, in the time since Jan had gotten engaged to Bob. The wedding presented a whole host of logistical problems, but it also touched on deeper questions—not just how her friendship with Jan would change once Jan was married, but whether her own life would ever change in the same way Jan's had.

And, of course, when Elaine thought of that question, she couldn't help but think of Nathan.

It wasn't that she wanted a wedding of her own, let alone one like Jan's seemed to be turning out to be. Her first wedding had been everything she had ever dreamed. And so had her first marriage, even with all of its little imperfections.

And it wasn't that she wanted to marry Nathan that instant. She loved dating Nathan, and she was actually tickled at the idea of being someone's girlfriend at her age—she would never in a million years have predicted such a thing. But at the same time, she couldn't see herself just "going steady" with Nathan for years on end. Neither she nor Nathan were people who liked to live in limbo. Probably she'd always known that at some point they'd either get married, or let each other go.

But the preparations for Jan's wedding had made that much clearer. And although Elaine prided herself on keeping a level head about things, weighing all the options and trusting God to bring her something good out of whatever came her way, when she tried to think of the future, she discovered she could only think of the future with Nathan. She made attempts, from time to time, to think about what life would be like without him, but it simply didn't work. It wasn't that the idea threw her into a tizzy of worry or sorrow. It was just that, whenever she thought of her own future, she imagined him there too.

Which couldn't help but make her wonder what it would be like to be married to him. She'd dated other men before she married: some briefly, like Jim Biggers, but nobody as seriously as Ben, whom she then married. But although she and Ben had been serious about each other from the beginning, the difference between dating and marriage was night and day. There were simply some things that you couldn't find out about a person, or yourself, until you pledged your life to them. No matter how much time you spent together, the whole game changed when both of your lives were on the line.

It had been years now since she lived with Ben. And although she enjoyed Jan's company and friendship now, their relationship wasn't a marriage. They were great partners, but when they wanted to, they went their separate ways. As Jan was about to do with Bob, in a very permanent way.

What would it be like to make that kind of commitment to another person at her age? Elaine wondered. When she'd married Ben, both of them had had to learn everything about marriage together, from scratch. She'd learned a lot of lessons with him, but what would it be like to try to build another marriage with another person, after all the years of life she'd already lived?

She took a deep breath of the crisp December air and smiled. Until now, she hadn't really thought through everything that was on her own mind when she thought about Nathan. With all this rattling around in there, it could very well be she who was acting strange and not Nathan.

But maybe, she thought, instead of calling him up, she should take a bit more time to work through her own feelings.

Her impromptu walk had brought her to the door of the Odyssey, the inventive restaurant that was always trying new flavors on the unsuspecting palates of the citizens of Lancaster. Its Christmas décor was no less inventive: what seemed like a waterfall of long, old-fashioned strands of tinsel fastened in an arch around the door. The material was classic, but the effect was electric, especially in the morning sun. She and Nathan often seemed to wind up at one of the town's other restaurants, perhaps because she liked Kate down at the diner so much, or perhaps just out of habit.

So this was exactly the kind of little luxury she should be enjoying in her single life, Elaine told herself: the chance to try out a promising menu item in a restaurant on a whim, just because she felt like it, without consulting anyone else.

And the sign outside was advertising hot honey cardamom cider. Elaine wasn't sure what that might taste like, but she was interested in finding out.

"For one?" the hostess asked when she stepped inside.

Elaine smiled and nodded, then followed the girl to a booth in the virtually empty restaurant, feeling very much like one of those characters in a movie who embarks on a trip in search of some distant wonderland. After all the traveling Elaine had done in her life with Ben, she wouldn't have thought she had any wanderlust in her. Which was not to say she didn't enjoy the little jolt of adventure and freedom.

But as she opened the menu to peruse the breakfast and lunch options, she heard a familiar voice.

Could it really be Nathan, or had she just been thinking of him so deeply that she'd started imagining things?

Over the booth she sat in was a larger mirror, facing the front of the restaurant, where she had just come in. And there, clearly reflected, was Nathan, with another woman. Nathan had just finished paying for their meal, and they were standing by the door, putting on their coats to leave.

At first, this didn't even give Elaine a pang. She simply looked curiously at the woman, trying to tell if she was one of Nathan's relatives, since she'd met everyone he was close to in his family, or even a client who she might recognize.

But as far as Elaine knew, she had never seen this woman before. She wasn't young enough to be a niece or a young cousin. Instead, she was around the same age as Elaine and Nathan, well-dressed, and pretty, with dark hair, a splash of red lipstick, and a string of understated pearls at her neck.

She looked like such an interesting person that Elaine started to rise in her seat, curious to meet her, and excited to say hello to Nathan. After everything she'd been thinking, maybe it was some kind of sign to find him here, where she least expected him, just when she'd thought she was so clever to go off on her own.

But as Elaine began to stand up, Nathan leaned down and gave the woman a kiss on the cheek. The woman responded by opening her arms and giving him a broad, expressive smile.

Nathan's greeting kiss could have just been a polite peck, but by now Elaine's guard was up, and it looked far too tender for her taste, although even in the moment she tried to tell herself that she was just being oversensitive. But as her heart began to speed up and her mind began to race, she realized that she'd never seen him kiss any other woman on the cheek.

And before she could calm herself down by making up some new explanation for what might be going on, the woman turned her head and kissed Nathan on the lips.

And in the same moment, before Elaine could look to see Nathan's reaction, Elaine suddenly realized that if she could see everything they were doing in the mirror, they could just as easily see her watching them. And right now, that sounded like the last thing in the world she wanted.

On the edge of the opposite side of her table, someone had left a copy of the *Penzance Courier.* Her face flushed and her heart pounding, Elaine picked it up and hid her face behind it.

CHAPTER THREE

When she lowered the paper again, the door was just thudding shut, and Nathan and the woman had vanished.

Elaine felt a lump in her throat and tears in her eyes.

You don't know what's going on, she told herself. *Calm down. There must be some explanation.*

But despite what her mind said, her heart continued to pound.

"Would you like to hear our specials?" the young waitress asked. She was blonde and perky, with turquoise rings on what seemed like every finger.

Elaine nodded, then completely failed to hear what the girl rattled off, as her own thoughts and feelings swirled around her.

"I'll have that," Elaine said.

The girl looked at her with surprise and something like admiration, and Elaine wondered wryly as she walked away what in the world she had just ordered for herself. Buffalo bacon? Fresh robin's eggs?

But when the girl left, Elaine was hit with a fresh wave of sickening worry. To fend it off, she looked down at the paper.

It had today's date, and that meant, she quickly realized, that it must contain the last installment of *The Crooked Lake Mystery.*

With relief for anything to distract her from the questions about Nathan that were now rolling through her head and troubling her heart, she opened the paper.

As she read the title of the installment, she felt a pang. She and Jan had agreed that they'd read the last one together. But if she told Jan what had just happened, Elaine thought, Jan would understand. She just needed to read a few lines, enough to settle her mind, and then she'd save the rest to share with Jan.

But when Elaine began to read, the story just pulled her in, as it always had. Maybe it was because she was so eager to forget the circumstances of her real life at that very moment. Or maybe it was just the power of the writing. But Elaine didn't look up again until the waitress brought her a bowl of cinnamon chili. And by that time, she was so close to the end that she couldn't stop herself from reading straight through.

In addition to being set in a town very much like Lancaster, the story was unusually compelling because it took place in the past, during the days when Elaine and Jan would have been girls. Elaine often read for escape and adventure, but there was extra pleasure in seeing through fresh eyes a place like the one in which you'd actually lived, and imagining new possibilities there.

But it was also unusual because the detective in the story had skin in the game. The basic mystery centered on the mysterious death of Helen, a student at the local high school. It was her lab partner, Jana, who led the informal investigation, after the town's police declared that her fall from a bridge was an accident. Unconvinced by this logic, because Helen had been a talented gymnast known her for grace and coordination, Jana began to look for clues for herself, even though the two of them hadn't been close during Helen's life.

Unlike in most mysteries, there weren't many possible suspects. In fact, at first, the problem was that there weren't any at all. Helen wasn't particularly popular, and she wasn't disliked. She wasn't especially smart, but she wasn't slow either. When Jana started asking people what they knew about her, hardly anyone seemed to remember her at all, not even the boy she had dated, who had already moved on with another girl, just weeks after Helen's death.

The pleasure of the mystery didn't come entirely from curiosity about whether Helen had been killed, and if so, who had done it. Instead, it came mostly from the discoveries Jana made about the town where she lived, and about Helen herself.

Chapter after chapter, the struggles and secrets of the people in the little town were revealed: the dreams the English teacher had once had of being a singer on Broadway, and the year she had spent in New York, when she had a child her husband never knew about. The paper bags of meat the butcher would leave on the porch of poor families under cover of darkness. The way the football player Helen had dated struggled to read, because of undiagnosed dyslexia, and the hours she had spent with him, reading passages from *The Scarlet Letter* or stories by Hemingway, or anything else their English teacher had assigned to them.

This last detail had given Elaine pause when she read it, because she remembered Jim Biggers asking her to read him a story aloud during the brief weeks they dated.

"I just like to hear the sound of your voice," he'd told her.

"Well, thank you," she said. "But wouldn't you like to hear me read something besides *Moby Dick*?"

The chapter he had asked her to read wasn't even one of the ones that contained the daring sea adventure story, but one of the interminable ones in which Melville simply went on and on about whales.

"It's interesting," Jim had insisted, and because it seemed harmless, Elaine had eventually given in—and learned far more than she had ever wanted to about the wide variety of whales in the known world.

It was especially strange to see that detail in a story that also contained a description of a car so much like Jim's. But people got to know each other right down to the last detail in small towns. Elaine just told herself that it wasn't so strange that a local writer might have known Jim and swiped a few of his stray characteristics. It didn't even mean that the character in the story was based on Jim. It could have simply been a matter of piling up lifelike details on the part of the writer.

But the real heart of the mystery was Helen.

Jana, the detective, had gone on the trail of the mystery for her own reasons, mainly because she couldn't believe that the shy, retiring girl she'd known as her lab partner would have ever been out on the bridge she'd fallen from, at night, all alone. And when people began to whisper at school that maybe it wasn't an accident, maybe Helen had jumped, Jana hadn't wanted to believe that either. During the course of the story, when lead after lead failed to pan out, Jana had even questioned herself.

But even as she began to uncover secrets she had never suspected among the people in the town where she had grown up, Jana still held on to a kernel of hope, that she hadn't been wrong about Helen. It wasn't that she didn't believe that bad things happened in the world, or that people could sometimes harm themselves or others. But it was Helen's hope that haunted her. When Helen had opened up to her over the lab counter, it had always been about Helen's dreams. Helen was quiet, but the things she hoped for in life were specific and vivid, and Jana couldn't believe that Helen would just put them at risk or throw them away, without a very good reason.

So the most compelling part of the mystery was Helen herself. In the early chapters of the story, Elaine had actually been a little impatient with the character of Helen, because she seemed so flat and nondescript. The only thing that had kept her attention was Jana's own curiosity and pluck, and the interesting revelations she began to uncover about her small town. But as the story unfolded, it was Helen who stole the stage, even from beyond the grave. And she stole it precisely because everyone who knew her seemed to have believed that she was so flat and nondescript, when in fact as the story progressed, it became clear that she had been so much more than anyone around her ever recognized.

It was true that she didn't have many friends at the high school she attended. But as Jana began to dig into her life, she discovered that Helen had touched many lives. She had visited an elderly woman who lived next door to her regularly, and she had become good friends with the seven-year-old boy who lived across the street and who struggled with being shy, just as she did. She was an excellent seamstress, so good that nobody at school ever knew that she sewed all her own clothes, although some people guessed that she must have some money and be traveling to the best shops in Boston in order to get the styles that nobody else in the school ever had. She read voraciously, not only the romances or novels that other girls her age read, but the encyclopedia and books of poetry. And because she loved to spend time with her father, she was a talented mechanic, which actually turned out to be a clue in the mystery: when the police found her car near the bridge, they assumed she had started to walk across the rickety old structure after a breakdown, but Jana believed Helen would have just popped the hood and fixed it herself.

The only person in the school who seemed to have any idea of Helen's depth was her football-playing boyfriend, Jon. And because of her shyness, even the two of them might not have ever wound up dating if they hadn't spent the summer working together at a farm stand just outside town. Just like everyone else, Jon hadn't thought much of Helen until the two of them got to talking. But when they did, he was both fascinated and charmed. So for the early part of the year, the two of them had been inseparable, despite the consternation of his buddies on the football team, and many of the other girls in school, who thought he was one of the great catches in the junior class.

But Jon was a high school boy, and after Helen's loss, his attention had wandered to Laney, a more popular girl. Jan and Elaine had spent some time debating whether Jon was the killer, but they hadn't been able to come up with a motive. Much as it was infuriating to watch how he had thrown Helen's affection aside, the problem with Jon was that he didn't seem to care deeply about Helen—just enough to date her casually, let alone want to harm her. And in the chapters leading up to the end, they'd discovered he had an iron-clad alibi, although he hadn't wanted to admit it originally, because he thought it was embarrassing: he'd been dressed up as a fairy that night, to help celebrate the birthday of his little sister, who had demanded a fairy-themed birthday party.

Through all of this, however, the character of Helen stood out, a quiet surface hiding untold depths. The story made Elaine and Jan curious about what had happened to Helen, and why. But its real lesson was to make them think twice about everyone they might otherwise look past in life: the quiet girl in school, the shy man at church, the clerk at the store whom it was all too easy to treat almost like a robot. Every one of them, the mystery reminded readers, was a full human being too, with dreams and wishes, friends and family, their own history, and their own hopes.

Elaine had picked up the story, eager to finally put an end to one small source of uncertainty in her life: the answer to the mystery. Because the writer had done such a beautiful job of building the world of Crooked Lake, she expected a satisfying conclusion, probably with a good-hearted message, that would tie everything up and put the world back to rights again.

But as she read through the final chapter of *The Crooked Lake Mystery,* the feeling of unease Elaine had been trying to shake after seeing Nathan with the other woman only grew.

By the final pages, after the waitress had delivered her meal, Elaine discovered that she'd absentmindedly devoured it, while scanning the last few columns, without even really tasting a bite.

The basic ending of the story was simple, even predictable. It turned out that Laney, Jon's new girlfriend, had actually been interested in him for years. Her feelings had become something of an obsession with her, and when he came back to school at the beginning of their junior year dating Helen, she had been shocked—then furious. So unbeknownst to her more popular friends, she had embarked on a plan of befriending Helen, pumping her for information about Jon, and hoping to break up the relationship by giving Helen bad advice.

But when that failed, Laney had resorted to more extreme measures. She had asked Helen to meet her on the bridge, planning just to scare her into breaking up with Jon. But to Laney's surprise, Helen had fought back, and in the ensuing struggle, Laney had accidentally pushed Helen off the bridge, into the raging waters below.

The story ended with a scene of Jon, confronting Laney after Jana cracked the case by reading Laney's diary, which contained a blow-by-blow description of both her passion for Jon and her plans for Helen. His sorrow over the loss of

Helen was touching, and so was his regret about everything he wouldn't be able to share with her now.

None of that would have done much more than give Elaine a pleasant sense of satisfaction and completion, if it hadn't been for the details of Laney's story.

Until this chapter, Laney had always been a tertiary character: there, but not central, the way any good mystery writer would introduce a suspect, then let them slip by the reader's attention until the reveal at the very end. Elaine only really remembered her because Jan had commented once on one of her descriptions.

"Didn't you have a skirt like that back in high school?" she asked. "Remember, that purple mohair, with the beautiful silver pinstripe?"

Elaine hadn't thought much of it at the time, but in the final chapter, there were half a dozen details about Laney that were uncomfortably similar to Elaine herself. Laney played field hockey, a sport Elaine had played herself in high school. Laney excelled in French, which had been one of Elaine's favorite subjects—and a surprisingly good preparation for all the years she spent abroad when she was married to Ben. Those might just have been stray details, but in this chapter, Jana surprised Laney in her favorite spot to go and think: a corner of the school library in a gable overlooking the schoolyard below.

When Elaine read this, the hair on the back of her neck began to stand up. As far as she knew, she had never told anybody about that spot. Even Jan might not know about it. She had never invited anyone to join her there, or asked anyone to meet her there, or even run into anyone else while she was taking a quiet moment on her own. It had been something she just kept to herself, during days that were otherwise crowded with the noise and chatter of other students.

The Laney character even wore a dainty gold watch, like the one Elaine's mother had given her for her sixteenth birthday, which she was still wearing on her wrist now.

Elaine set the paper down beside her now-empty bowl. She had come into Odyssey looking for just what she had been hoping for all those years ago when she snuck away for a moment in the library gable: a moment alone, to collect herself and listen to her own thoughts.

She couldn't believe everything that had happened since she sat down in that booth, even though all she had done was glance around the place and read an article in the paper.

But as she turned the strange similarities between the Laney character and herself over in her mind, she realized there was another one. Even the character's name was similar to hers. In fact, there had been a brief attempt while she was in high school to give her the nickname Laney. That had happened so long ago that she barely remembered it. It came up from the deepest depths of her memory reluctantly but soon joined a host of details, the pleasant teasing of high school kids, back and forth, their laughter and innocence.

Could the name of the Laney character be another coincidence? she wondered. Or, paired with all the details about Jim, had it been written by someone who knew both of them?

She looked down at the dainty gold watch on her wrist, which patiently ticked off minute after minute, as it had for so many years before, all kinds of details and questions swirling in her head.

But as she watched the minute hand swing slowly over the face of the clock, the deeper question finally surfaced. If it was true that the Laney character was based on her, why in the world would the author have made her into a murderer? Had there been someone in her life in high school who disliked her that much? And were they still nursing a grudge so deep, after all this time?

CHAPTER FOUR

Is everything all right?" the waitress asked as she picked up the check.

Elaine hesitated, not sure how to answer.

After a moment, she just smiled.

The girl answered with a bright smile of her own, checked the cash Elaine had put inside, and looked back at Elaine with wide eyes.

"Thank *you,*" she said.

Elaine shook her head as the girl walked away, wondering what mistake she must have made with the change. She believed in tipping well, especially for good service, but she hadn't meant to leave an amount big enough to get that kind of reaction.

Sighing, she swept the copy of the *Penzance Courier* into her purse, then headed for the door. A few steps before she reached it, the phone in her bag began to ring.

When she saw Jan's familiar face on the screen, she felt a sense of relief. She'd have to confess, of course, that she'd read the end of the story without Jan, but she knew her cousin well enough to know that small crime would immediately be forgiven as soon as she told Jan all the strange details that appeared in the story.

Then maybe Jan could bring some sense to the situation. Perhaps it would all look like coincidence to her. Perhaps Jan would even remember there were other girls in school with similar watches, or extracurricular activities. Perhaps all these years, she had been sharing the library nook she thought was just her own with some other sympathetic soul.

And in any case, it would be good to get someone else's perspective on the story—especially Jan, because Elaine knew that no matter what anyone else ever thought about her, good or bad, her cousin would still be on her side.

"Jan," she said when she answered, on a note of relief.

But Jan's tone when she spoke was even more full of relief than Elaine's. "Elaine," she said, her voice slightly high with stress. "Thank God you answered."

Elaine's heart skipped a beat. What else could have possibly happened today that hadn't happened already? she wondered. But as she did, a whole host of other disasters slid through her mind. She might be feeling overwhelmed by the day's events, but things could definitely be worse. What in the world was Jan worried about now? Something serious, or another wedding false alarm?

"I need butter," Jan told her.

"Butter?" Elaine repeated. As the main bookkeeper for the tearoom, she happened to know that Jan should be quite well stocked with butter. It was one of the expenses that always made Elaine wince a bit each week as she tallied it up. But Jan insisted that there was no other ingredient that could be substituted to make her exquisite scones. Nobody, not even Elaine, could argue with Jan's scones. But she did happen to know that several pounds of butter had been purchased for the tearoom kitchen within the past two days. "How much butter?"

"Oh, not too much," Jan said. "I'd say, maybe ten or twenty pounds."

Elaine's eyes widened. That would be another big expense, and not one that she'd been expecting in their budget, although it wouldn't break the bank.

"I thought you were almost done making those scones," she said, trying to keep her tone light and encouraging, because Jan obviously hadn't broken out of her mood from that morning.

"I am," Jan said. "I just want to try one thing more."

"Maybe I could just bring you a few pounds, then," Elaine suggested. "As a sample."

"No, no." Jan's voice rose in agitation. "That won't work. I don't just need to test how they taste. I need to practice making the whole batch. There are all kinds of surprises when you double and triple things. And I'm going to be making five or six times the recipes for this party. I've already cut that by half."

"All right, all right," Elaine said, hoping her tone might help soothe Jan back to her normal sensible self.

"Bring me nine pounds." Jan sounded as if Elaine had bargained her into a corner. "I can make three batches with that."

"I'm on my way," Elaine said, but the line had already gone dead as Jan turned her attention back to the ongoing fray in the tearoom kitchen.

Elaine took a deep breath as she slid into her car and headed toward the grocery store. Maybe this was just what she needed: a simple, mundane task to ground her back in the details of daily life and help her to let go of all the imagination and speculation currently swirling through her head, about everything from her high school days to the woman she'd seen earlier that morning with Nathan.

And she was right. By the time she got to the grocery store, she felt much more like herself. It was pleasant to walk through the aisles with only one item on her list, rather than with a head crowded with which items she had to make sure not to forget in which aisle. The sight of the familiar products on the shelves, orderly and abundant, was always soothing to her, a sign that in at least one place, everything was just as it should be. And she was glad to have a task at hand that she knew without question she could accomplish. Even if she couldn't figure out what to do about seeing Nathan that morning or figure out what the story in the paper had to do with her, if anything, she could at least buy a few pounds of butter and take them home.

By the time she reached the checkout line, arms full of brightly colored boxes of butter, she was feeling much better.

And when she heard a familiar voice say her name from behind her in line, she turned around, delighted.

"Bianca," she said, when she caught sight of Bianca Stadler's smiling face.

Bianca lifted her arms, which were covered in her trademark jangling gold bracelets—and filled with boxes of cornstarch. "Looks like you're also making a restaurant run. Out of butter in the kitchen?"

"I guess so," Elaine said ruefully.

"It's amazing what a business can run through between grocery orders," Bianca said. "I would have sworn we got an industrial-sized pack of this stuff last week, but Mel tells me we're out, and also that we can't get through another night until the next order comes tomorrow without another ten boxes."

"Tell me about it," Elaine said. "I'm not sure what happens to butter in our kitchen. Sometimes I think maybe we must be supporting a whole civilization of mice who only live on butter."

Even as she spoke, she felt a wistful tug. Getting rid of a passel of mice would be a whole lot easier than the real source of the problem, which was Jan's love for expensive ingredients—and these days, all her nervous energy about the upcoming wedding. Neither of those could be dealt with by a quick visit from a good exterminator.

Bianca grinned, her long dark hair falling back over her shoulders. "I know it's all Mel's fault. I'm just not sure what he does with all this cornstarch. I asked him the other day if he was giving it out to the football team, to draw the white lines on the field."

"I think you might need even more boxes if that's the case," Elaine said with a smile.

The two of them scooted up as one of the customers in front of them stepped up to the clerk with their selections, but it was still early in the day, so not many of the lanes were open. As always seemed to be the case, the express line was moving much slower than the others.

"I was just thinking of you this morning," Bianca went on.

"Oh, really?" Elaine was pleasantly surprised. Bianca was a solid, kind soul, and it was lovely to hear that she'd been on her mind.

"Yes," Bianca said. "When I picked up a copy of today's *Penzance Courier*."

Suddenly, all the good feelings Elaine had built up on her drive to the store vanished, replaced by a chunk of heavy dread in her stomach and a prickle of worry that ran over the back of her shoulders.

"Oh?" Elaine responded, warily. At the same time, she tried to calm herself. There was no reason for her to believe that Bianca had noticed the same details she had in the story. After all, they were such personal details that almost nobody else but Elaine would have noticed them. That was, if Bianca had even been reading the serialized mystery. She could be talking about something completely different.

"Have you been reading *The Crooked Lake Mystery*?" Bianca asked in a confiding voice. "I don't think I've talked to anyone in town who hasn't. It's just so good."

Queasily, Elaine nodded. "Jan and I have been enjoying it." At least until the final chapter, she thought.

"I've thought of you several times as I was reading it," Bianca said. "You remember that old candy apple–red car of Jim's? I just remember you looking out from it when he drove you home after school, with your big movie star sunglasses and your hair blowing in the wind."

Elaine tried to smile. She barely remembered dating Jim—they'd only spent a few weeks together, as she recalled, but apparently it had made an impression on Bianca. And on who else? she wondered. “That was a beautiful car,” she said.

Bianca nodded enthusiastically.

“And not just the car,” she said. “Do you remember that little blue jacket you used to wear, our junior year? The one with the rickrack border?”

Until that moment, Elaine hadn’t remembered. But now that Bianca mentioned it, it sprang up full-blown in her memory. It had actually been a hand-me-down from one of her distant cousins, whose parents had a much bigger budget than hers did to spend on clothes. It had cashmere in the blend, which made it the softest thing Elaine had ever owned until then, but to make it her own, she’d added a strip of inexpensive rickrack around the neck and sleeves, to give it some flair. “I remember that,” she said.

“I couldn’t help but think of you when I read the chapter about Laney adding lace to her jacket,” Bianca said.

That detail in the story hadn’t even caught Elaine’s attention until now, because it hadn’t seemed to mirror her own life at all.

“Hmm,” Elaine said.

“You were the only person in high school I ever knew to do anything like that, add your own touch to clothes you’d bought. Although in the story, Laney’s jacket is a hand-me-down.”

The pinpricks on the back of Elaine’s neck only intensified. She didn’t share the fact that her own jacket had been a hand-me-down with Bianca. But how had she missed that detail herself? And how many more details like it would pop out at her now, if she read the whole mystery from the beginning, with new eyes?

"And your mohair skirt!" Bianca exclaimed. "With the silver stripe in it! Who could forget that? I used to come up with plots during geography class about how I was going to swipe that skirt from you, during gym. I thought maybe you wouldn't notice if I swapped it out with my phys ed bloomers." She laughed, making it clear that she'd never actually been a threat to Elaine's skirt.

Elaine tried to laugh with Bianca, but her chest felt hollow. "I guess maybe I wasn't the only one in the world who had one of those skirts," she said, although she felt less and less sure that there was no connection between her and the character in the mystery with each passing moment.

"I don't know," Bianca said. "Were you up to some shenanigans none of the rest of us knew about in high school?"

By the warmth in Bianca's eyes, Elaine could see that she was only teasing, because Bianca was so sure that Elaine would never have done anything like the character in the story who bore such weird similarities to her former self. And she knew that nobody else in town would seriously think she was a criminal.

But Elaine still felt herself pulling her wrists farther into her jacket, to keep Bianca from catching sight of the gold watch her mother had given her and coming up with yet another connection between Elaine and the story.

"I think pretty much everyone was just doing their best to get through high school," Elaine said.

"Isn't that the truth." Bianca shook her head.

"Next!" called the cashier.

Elaine turned back. As they'd been talking, the customers ahead of them had quietly filed through the line, and now it was her turn.

"Great to see you," she said to Bianca as she stepped up with her gold bricks of butter.

"Always," Bianca said as Elaine checked out.

But while Elaine walked back out into the crisp air of the Lancaster winter toward her car, she couldn't shake the uneasy feeling Bianca's comments had given her.

She knew that nobody in town would ever believe the idea that she had been involved in any kind of a serious crime. But if Bianca had noticed some of the same similarities between Elaine and Laney that Elaine had, who else in town might notice—especially if, as Bianca said, everybody in town seemed to be devouring the story just the way Jan and Elaine had. What would they think if they did? Would they play it off as a joke? Would it plant unpleasant thoughts about Elaine in their heads?

And much more important, who in the world would ever have written a story in which Elaine was a villain? Was there somebody out there who saw Elaine as the villain in their own life? And if so, why?

Elaine shook her head and got into the car, realizing she was starting to spiral down into the same storm of thoughts she had just escaped during her time at the grocery store.

Maybe, she thought, she was just letting herself get stuck in these mental weeds because she was really, secretly, so thrown off balance by the interaction she had seen between Nathan and the mystery woman at the Odyssey.

That thought made her feel better, because there was something she could do about it, and because the thought of Nathan always made her feel better. With a little bit of distance, all the memories she'd built with him over the past few years flooded back. And not just over the past few years, but over the better part of both their lives, since the two of them had first become friends as kids, due to the bond their own fathers shared. She'd known Nathan, actually, since even before high school. If anyone would have any perspective on this whole thing with the mystery story and her personal details, it would be Nathan.

Feeling both eager and a little sheepish, Elaine pulled out her phone. She wasn't sure why she hadn't bothered to just call him before now and ask him directly what he had been up to that morning. In all the decades she'd known him, she'd never known him to lie to her. And she was sure there must be some explanation of the scene she'd seen earlier that morning, probably an interesting or a funny one.

As she turned up the heat in the car, she pressed his number on her favorites list and held the phone to her ear.

After a few rings, Nathan's familiar voice came on the line.

"Hi, honey," he said.

Was it just her, or did he sound busy and distracted and... not exactly happy to hear from her?

Elaine took a breath. Maybe reading that story in the paper had gotten under her skin more than she knew.

"Hey, Nathan," she said, suddenly feeling uncertain of what to say next, although in general the two of them loved to prattle on together about any little thing they'd seen or thought of that day. It was almost like she was a teenager again, trying to figure out how to have a conversation with this strange new breed called boys. "How is your morning going?"

"Oh," Nathan said, his voice trailing off as if she'd just asked him about something that required lengthy and complicated calculations. A moon shot, for instance.

Elaine's brow furrowed, wondering what in the world required the time he was taking.

"Oh," he said again, "it's fine."

Elaine's frown deepened even further at this. There was a strange note in his voice, one that she had never heard before. It sounded fake, although she wouldn't recognize that tone in him, since he was always so sincere as a rule. Or was it not so much fake as *untrue*?

"Really?" Elaine tried to keep a sharp note of alarm or accusation out of her own voice. "What have you been up to?"

"Uh...," Nathan said, and launched into another one of his new but epic pauses.

"Have I caught you at a bad time?" Elaine asked.

"Uh," Nathan repeated.

Then, in the background, Elaine heard the sound of a woman's voice. It wasn't one she recognized, and she couldn't make out the actual words that were being said, but she recognized the tone: teasing, with a bright confidence that bordered on...flirtation?

"Where are you?" Elaine demanded.

"Hey, listen, Elaine," Nathan said, "can I call you back? I'm right in the middle of something."

In the background, Elaine could hear the woman break into a peal of laughter.

Then, without waiting for an answer, he hung up the phone.

Elaine was so shocked that she bumped the horn of her car, the blare causing an older woman who was walking a friendly terrier on the sidewalk near Elaine to execute a startled hop.

The woman walked over and tapped Elaine's window. "Honey?" she queried as Elaine quickly rolled it down. The dog looked up at Elaine curiously. "You okay?"

"I'm sorry," Elaine said. "I just—I accidentally bumped the horn."

But as the woman smiled politely and continued her walk, her question echoed in Elaine's mind.

And she knew the answer. She wasn't okay. Not even close to it.

CHAPTER FIVE

Elaine listened outside the door of the kitchen for a minute for clues as to the state of things within.

The only thing she could hear was a steady swish, as if the kitchen were full of pines and wind had just begun to blow through them.

Cautiously, she cracked the door and stuck her head in.

To her surprise, the entire kitchen had returned to its neat-as-a-pin normal state, with the vast majority of the counters now spic-and-span, except for the one nearest the door, which was piled high with what looked to be a dozen plastic containers filled with scones, and the counter beside the sink where Jan stood with her back to the door, washing dishes. This space was piled even higher with pans, pots, bowls, spatulas, and all the other equipment Jan had put to work in pursuit of the perfect scone.

Elaine raised her bag of butter in the air as she entered, like a Scottish warlord lifting up his tribute to show he came in peace.

"Brought the butter!" she said brightly. It was a good sign that Jan had begun to clean up, or at least Elaine thought it was. But maybe she had only run out of steam because she had run out of ingredients. Would introducing more butter to the situation set off another storm of baking?

But Jan just gave a brief nod and turned back to the sink, where she was now washing dishes with all the fire and determination with which she had been producing scones a few hours ago.

Elaine walked over and set the butter down on the counter nearby, as unobtrusively as possible, she hoped.

"Oh, you can just put that in the fridge," Jan said. "I'll use it tomorrow."

Elaine didn't need to be told twice. Quickly she stashed the boxes of butter in their big fridge, in the back behind a carton of milk, where it was out of sight and hopefully couldn't provoke any more trouble.

"Thanks for getting that," Jan said. "I just decided, this is crazy. What was I thinking, baking another three dozen scones?"

Elaine cocked her eye toward the dozens piled up neatly on the counter and wondered at exactly what threshold that thought had finally kicked in. It obviously wasn't after the *first* three dozen scones. Or the second. Or the third.

"How are you doing?" Jan asked.

Elaine looked at her cousin. Despite her descent into wedding scone madness that morning, the old Jan she knew and loved seemed to have returned. Instead of a look of worry and drive, her face was just as open and observant as ever. And as

Jan looked at Elaine this time, her own brow furrowed. "Are you all right?" she asked. "What happened?"

Elaine's mind flashed quickly back to the moment she had seen the woman in the restaurant kiss Nathan, but she couldn't bring herself to put that into words. Maybe she didn't want to believe it was even true, although she had no question that what she had seen was real. Or maybe some loyal part of her didn't want to smear his name before she understood all the facts.

But she knew she needed to give Jan an answer. And the incident with Nathan wasn't the only thing on her mind. But to tell that story, she'd have to begin by admitting she'd finished the story she and Jan had been reading together.

"I've got a confession to make," Elaine said, a smile twitching on her lips.

Jan raised her eyebrows as she dropped a newly clean colander into the increasingly overloaded dish drainer. "Okay. Out with it."

"Well," Elaine said, "I went to lunch and found today's *Penzance Courier* at the restaurant." Sheepishly, she pulled it out of her purse and laid it on the nearby counter.

As usual, Jan's mind was quick to grasp the situation. Almost before Elaine had finished talking, her eyes narrowed in understanding.

"You read the ending," she said, then turned her chin up in mock indignation. "I think we're done here."

"I know," Elaine said. "I know we promised to read it together. And I'm sorry. But—"

Jan started laughing, unable to keep her act up any longer. She shook her head. "I understand. Don't worry about it. If you put a copy of the ending of that story in front of me, I can't make any claim that I wouldn't have done exactly the same thing."

She switched the water off, pushed her hair back off her forehead, and leaned on the counter, clearly taking the time to give Elaine her undivided attention.

"So," she said, "how was it?"

At the look on Elaine's face, her expression changed from eagerness to concern.

"That bad?" she asked.

As Elaine paused, still struggling to find the words to say, Jan came over and slid her arm around Elaine's waist and gave her a comforting squeeze.

"It's not just the story," she guessed, "is it?"

"Well," Elaine said, "it is and it isn't."

Haltingly, she began to explain all the similarities between her and the Laney character: the penchant for altering clothes, the library nook, even the name.

"I never knew you hid up there in the library."

"Nobody did," Elaine said. "That was the whole point of it. It was only my place."

"I understand that," Jan said. "I used to go into the pantry in the home ec room from time to time, just to take a breath and collect myself. There's always so much going on in any day at high school, and all of it can seem like the end of the world."

Elaine nodded. "But how did it end up in the story?"

Jan patted Elaine's shoulder, but with an air that suggested Elaine might be reacting a bit like a teenager to the situation. "I don't know. But what does it matter if a few details about your life wound up in a story by a local writer? I would think that's actually to be expected. You could even take it as a compliment."

"A compliment?" Elaine yelped. "But Laney is the murderer!"

The quick change of shock in Jan's expression made her realize that not only had she not shared that detail with Jan yet, she had just inadvertently ruined the story for her.

"Oh no," she said. "I'm sorry. I didn't mean to—"

But Jan's mind was already spinning off in some other direction. "Not the English teacher?" she asked. "I thought for sure it was the English teacher." Her brows knit in dislike. "Anyone who's always correcting her colleagues' grammar like that..."

Then her face changed again, into indignation. "All those details you just told me," she said. "All those details of *your* life. You're telling me the author used them for the *murderer*?"

Elaine nodded. Finally, she felt like she wasn't crazy. Jan was just about as upset as she had been herself.

"What's the name of this writer again?" Jan asked, snatching for the paper on the counter.

"It's just a pen name," Elaine said as Jan scanned for the title page of the serialized story.

"How do you know that?" Jan asked as she flipped to the right page and read... "Joy T. T. World."

"Joy To The World," Elaine said, in a weary voice. "Pretty sure there's no one anyone in the Lancaster area with that name."

She expected Jan to drop the paper back to the counter and give the problem of her stolen personal details her full attention, but to her irritation, Jan was squinting at the left-hand margin of the story, reading down the column, just as she had with the earlier editions of the story.

Elaine gave a sigh of dissatisfaction and crossed her arms. Jan's obsession with this nonexistent code had seemed like a cute quirk in the past few weeks. But at a time like this, when Elaine was trying to reckon with actual facts, it made her feel as though Jan wasn't taking something that felt very serious to her very seriously at all.

"Look at this," Jan said.

Instead, Elaine looked at the ceiling. Jan had found several words in the past few weeks: *year, sorry, holiday, white,* but none of them seemed to add up to anything like a cogent message—not to mention the fact that, in Elaine's opinion, random words must show up in columns of letters that long all the time.

"You found another word?" Elaine asked, her voice markedly unenthusiastic. So what if she'd found a *dolphin* or a *cupcake*? She couldn't imagine any word that would make the collection Jan already thought she had discovered make any more or less sense than they already did. Or didn't.

Jan nodded. *"Meet,"* she said.

Meet was one of the shortest words Jan had "discovered" yet. Obviously a stroke of random chance, Elaine thought.

But then Jan raised her head, her eyes shining. "And there's more!"

"More?" Elaine asked.

Jan nodded and pointed to the paper.

Curious despite herself, Elaine leaned up against the counter beside Jan and peered down at the crackling paper as Jan's finger trailed down the column.

There, just as she'd said, was the word *meet,* clearly spelled out in the vertical of the far left of the column.

But below it was another word.

"Sea," Elaine read.

"And," Jan prompted, her finger still traveling down the column.

"Pine," Elaine read, and her own eyes skipped ahead, looking for the familiar word she knew should come next. *"Park,"* she read.

"Sea Pine Park," Jan said.

The cousins' eyes locked. Sea Pine Park was small and a bit out of the way, but it was well known to the residents of Lancaster, a beautiful little scrap of land on the banks of Chickadee Lake, with a small parking area, play area, and benches, and nothing else to obscure the natural beauty of the spot.

"It's setting a meeting place," Jan said, her voice breathy with excitement. "And look at this."

Her finger stabbed at the text just below the four lines that spelled out *park.*

"Five," she said. "*OC.* That must stand for five o'clock. Someone's setting up a meeting."

"In the local paper?" Elaine kept her voice skeptical, although she could feel her own heart begin to race too. "Why wouldn't they just make a phone call? Or send a text?"

"I don't know," Jan said, her eyes wide with delight. "But you don't think *this* is still a random coincidence, do you?"

"No," Elaine admitted. Her eyes skipped forward again, looking for more words as she read aloud. *"C-E-P-T-T-J-A-E. . . "* She trailed off as any further pattern stubbornly refused to emerge.

"There's nothing else there," Jan said. "That I can find."

"Five o'clock when?" Elaine asked.

Jan grinned like a kid at Christmas. "I don't know!" she said.

Elaine shook her head, as if that action might just make every strange thing that had happened that day fall into place and finally make sense. It didn't.

"What do you think it means?" Elaine asked.

"If we find out," Jan said, "maybe it will tell us something about who the author is. And what in the world they were doing using details from your life in this story."

"You think they're from my life?" Elaine asked. "You don't think it's just coincidence?"

"I don't think these letters are coincidence," Jan said, pointing at the strange message that trailed down the newspaper page. "And I don't think the details in the story are, either."

She looked back up at the title of the story and the pseudonym below. "Joy T.T. World," she mused. "I wonder if you've ever written anything else."

"That's a good thought," Elaine said eagerly. "Maybe they have a website. Or even bookstore events."

Her skin tingled at the idea of stepping into a bookstore reading and looking up at the front of the room to see the face of whoever it was who had stolen the details of her history. Because that's what it felt like to her—stealing. It wasn't as if someone had taken money from her purse, but in some ways it was worse. Even more personal.

Jan had already reached for the laptop that Elaine had left stashed on a kitchen counter after the last time she used it.

"Do you mind?" she asked.

Elaine shook her head as Jan opened the computer, waited for the screen to come up, and then started a web browser and typed in *Joy T.T. World.*

The search turned up only a few hits, mostly arrangements of Christmas music.

"Try *Joy T.T. World, author,*'" Elaine suggested.

This brought the search returns down to virtually nothing.

"How about just *Joy World*?" Elaine tried.

When Jan typed it in, the screen exploded with inspirational tchotchkes: posters, stuffed animals, T-shirts, journals . . . but no author photos.

"Maybe *Joy World, author*?" Jan guessed, typing as she spoke.

This time, the screen filled with YouTube arrangements of the old carol, maps of the globe, a smattering of world music, and a still-significant collection of inspirational junk.

Jan sighed.

"I can't believe there's no trace at all," Elaine said. "The story seems quite professional. It's hard to believe whoever wrote it has never published before."

"Well, Emily Dickinson never published a single poem in her lifetime. And there's no question she knew how to write."

"That's true," Elaine mused. "You know what?" she said suddenly. "Check the website for the *Penzance Courier.*"

Jan navigated to the site of the hometown paper, then looked back over her shoulder at her cousin.

"Now what?" she asked.

"Do they have the serialized story online? Maybe there's a link to an author page," Elaine said.

Quickly, Jan typed *Crooked Lake Mystery* into the search bar for the paper. Both cousins held their breath for the brief moment that the search engine ground through the options, looking for their return. Then they both gasped in elation as the title came up.

"Bingo!" Jan said as she clicked through it.

But when the page came up, with the text of the very first episode of the serialization, and a list down the side of the screen naming all the following chapters, the author's name was in simple text, not hyperlinked.

Jan clicked on it anyway.

"It doesn't lead to anything," Elaine said, her eyes sliding over the memorable first lines of the text that had drawn her, Jan, and so many of the other residents of Lancaster into the remarkable story.

> Everyone in town thought they knew what had happened to Helen Pendergrast.
>
> But Jana Warren knew they must be wrong.

"I know it doesn't," Jan said, her shoulders slumping. "But I was hoping I was wrong."

She turned back from the computer and slid her arm around Elaine's waist again.

"I'm sorry," she said. "This has only ever been an interesting mystery to me. But to you, it must feel so strange."

"It does," Elaine agreed.

"Do you think there's any connection between the code and the details about your life in the story?" Jan asked. "Does any of it mean anything to you?"

"The words you found before?" Elaine suggested thoughtfully. *"Year, holiday."*

"And *sorry,"* Jan added.

Elaine nodded. That one had been on her mind, but she hadn't liked to say it. Did somebody think she should be sorry for something? Or was it a threat, that one day she would *be* sorry?

"Year, holiday," she repeated. "I don't think they mean much more to me than anyone else."

"What about *white*?" Jan asked. "Do you know anyone by that name?"

"I think everybody probably knows somebody by that name," Elaine said uneasily. Because apparently, by the evidence of all the personal details included in the story, at least one person she didn't know had gotten closer to her than she had ever suspected.

"What about Sea Pine Park?" Jan asked. "Do you have any connection with it?"

"I don't think so," Elaine said, trying without success to dig any special memories at the park out of her memory. She had played there as a little girl, she knew, but she didn't remember doing anything much more than walking past it since she was grown—not even during her teen years, which seemed to be the focus of the details in the story.

Jan stared down at the paper, tracing her finger over the entirety of the front page. Then, suddenly, she looked up, her eyes bright.

"You know who *must* know?" she said.

"Who?" Elaine asked.

"The paper," Jan said. "There's no way they could have published this without knowing *something* about the identity of the author. Even if the writer used a pen name when they submitted it, they have to have some way to communicate. At least an e-mail address..."

"The *Penzance Courier* still pays its writers," Elaine said. She remembered this fact because she'd been pleasantly surprised to receive a check after writing a brief article about tea ceremonies a few years back, when the tearoom had just opened. She'd done it just for the sake of publicity for the business, but had been gratified to receive enough to treat herself to a small pair of antique earrings she'd found in the days after the article was published. "So they must have some kind of mailing address."

"Hmm," Jan said. "You know, one of the things I've had on my list is to finally get a picture over there for our engagement announcement. If we wait too much longer, we'll be married before they even report the fact that we're engaged."

She scooped up her purse and began to root through a stack of papers on the counter until she came up with a recent snapshot of her and Bob, looking, Elaine thought, even happier than many young couples she'd seen announcing their own engagements in the paper.

"I'll take it over right now," Jan said. "And while I'm there, I'll talk to River and see what I can find out."

Elaine raised her eyebrows. "Good luck with that." River White, at the *Courier*, was a dogged reporter, known for ruffling feathers around town with his take-no-prisoners interview style.

"I'll give him a dose of his own medicine," Jan said, and winked as she went out.

CHAPTER SIX

Jan sighed with satisfaction as she stepped through the doors of the *Penzance Courier.*

Even the newsroom wasn't exempt from the Christmas spirit. A fake evergreen wreath with a big red bow dangled improbably from the ceiling fan in the middle of the room, twinkle lights ran along the front desk, and a half-eaten tray of homemade Christmas cookies welcomed any guests, apparently free for all.

For some reason, Jan had always felt drawn to newspapers. She loved to read books and watch shows about reporters on the beat, and one of her favorite classic movies was *His Girl Friday,* about the high jinks of a girl reporter trying to nail down a big story—although it probably didn't hurt that the romantic lead was Cary Grant.

And when she'd homeschooled her kids, one of her favorite units, aside from science, had been journalism. She loved combing through the papers with them, teaching them how different news items appeared in the different sections, watching how a story broke one day and then was followed up on over the next days, or weeks.

She even enjoyed teaching them the nitty-gritty details of how a newspaper article was organized, which was very different than the way she taught them to write essays. An essay was balanced, doling out ideas piece by piece, leading up to a big conclusion. But in a newspaper article, the conclusion came first. The idea was to make sure that busy people could get the gist of an important story, even if they only had the time to glance at it.

That too was very different, she reflected, from how most people got their news these days, from TV or over the Internet. Those media weren't focused on getting the facts of a story across as quickly as possible. They were interested in making sure viewers or readers kept watching or clicking—even if it meant burying the details of a story after a long string of lead-ins or advertisements, and writing enticing headlines that didn't really tell the truth, to keep people titillated and in their seats.

In any case, she certainly got a good dose of journalistic flavor walking through the door of the *Penzance Courier.* The place might have been built to specifications directly from the set of *His Girl Friday,* with exposed brick walls, giant windows that faced the street in front, and desks lining the walls of the large open floor plan.

And, Jan thought with a little zing of satisfaction, she was there to do a bit of reporting herself today. And not just on any story. On a story that seemed to have something to do with the newspaper itself.

As she approached the desk, a woman looked up. She was about Jan's age, with sandy caramel-colored curls, merry green eyes, and a bright splash of pink lipstick. At the sight of Jan, she broke into a big smile.

"Hi, Jan!" she said. "Well, it's been a month of Sundays since I've seen you. Maybe more than a month!"

"Hi, Cookie," Jan said.

Cookie's eye drifted to the ring sparkling on Jan's finger.

"Jan!" she squealed. "Are you...?"

Half-embarrassed, half-thrilled, Jan nodded.

"Oh my goodness," Cookie said, rising from her seat to clutch Jan's hand and inspect the ring. "Oh, it's beautiful. Now who in the world...?"

"Bob," Jan said, when Cookie's eyes met hers. As she always seemed to do now when she said his name, she broke into a wide smile. And this time, she didn't even bother trying to hide it.

"Bob?" Cookie repeated.

"Bob Claybrook." Jan felt a slight tingle at the fact that his last name would soon be hers.

"Oh, he's the nicest man," Cookie said. "Isn't he just the nicest man?"

"Well, I think so," Jan said with a little twist of her lips.

"And how is the wedding planning going?" Cookie asked as she took her seat again. She leaned forward in anticipation, as if she'd just gotten to the good part of the movie.

"Oh," Jan said, looking heavenward.

"I know! I know! Isn't it crazy? Everybody always wants you to do so much, but I just kept telling them, I want to keep it simple. Just simple, simple. After all, this wasn't the first time down the aisle for either of us. It's not like we need to have a three-ring circus. I figured," Cookie said, "the real miracle was even just finding love again at this time in life. Anything else was just gilding the lily. But try telling them that!" she exclaimed. "I bet you're having that same problem, aren't you?" she asked. "Everyone wanting to make it more complicated than it has to be."

Jan felt a twinge of frustration. Actually, she'd heard the "keep it simple" message again and again, from just about everybody in her life. But what if she didn't want to keep it simple? Cookie was right about one thing: starting a new life with Bob did feel like a miracle to her. And what if she wanted to celebrate, and celebrate in style? What was wrong with that?

But instead of saying all this aloud, Jan just smiled.

"Well, I hope you can help me keep one thing simple," she said, pulling out the picture of her and Bob she'd brought with her. "I think it's about time we got our announcement in the paper, seeing as how the wedding is coming up soon."

Cookie took the picture from her and grinned down at it. "Well, isn't that lovely. You two look like a couple of teenagers in love. Look at those smiles. And you," she said, looking up at Jan. "You look absolutely gorgeous."

Jan would never have used that word to describe herself, but her discomfort melted quickly in the warmth of Cookie's compliment. Love did funny things to people, she thought. She certainly felt as though it had transformed parts of her life. And maybe, somehow, that showed up in the picture too.

Cookie took the photo in hand and opened the low door in the counter to let Jan pass into the newsroom, which Jan did with a little pang of excitement.

"Right this way," she said. "You're in luck. Candace Huang handles these announcements, and she's in this afternoon. She'll just need to get a few details from you and then she can write up the article in time for next week's engagement announcements. We only do those once a week, so your timing is perfect."

"Wonderful," Jan said. She and Elaine had both had good experiences working with Candace before. She was unfailingly friendly and ready to help—almost the exact opposite of the experiences they'd had with her fellow reporter, River White, who, though his heart was usually in the right place, in general came off as pushy and aggressive.

When they stopped at Candace's desk, Candace looked up. "Jan," she said. "It's good to see you. I bet you've got some kind of interesting story for me today."

"I'll say she does," Cookie said as she handed over the photograph of Bob. "But this won't be an investigative piece. It's going in the Weddings section."

When Candace looked back up, her face was all smiles. "Have a seat," she told Jan. "I'm looking forward to hearing this story—and telling it."

As Cookie returned to her place by the door, Jan sat down with Candace, near the center of the newsroom.

"So," Candace said, clicking through several files on her computer, "let me just start by getting some basic information from you."

Quickly, she took Jan and Bob's formal names, the names of the family members they wanted included in the announcement, and the wedding date.

At the mention of the date, Candace looked up from her computer screen. "That's coming soon," she observed.

Jan felt a familiar tightening around her chest. "I don't think anybody knows that better than I do," she said, trying to smile.

"Jitters are normal." Candace gave her a kindly look.

"I'm not sure I'd call them jitters," Jan said. She had had jitters with her first marriage, because the whole idea was so incredibly new. She had barely lived back then and she had no idea what she was getting herself into. Today, she felt she understood at least something about marriage. "It's more like a planning challenge," Jan said. "One thing I knew for sure was that I wanted a tea to be part of our celebration. A real one, with some true scones, some elements of the classic English tea service, and possibly some other traditions. So I'm planning a wedding tea in lieu of a rehearsal dinner."

Her shoulders drooped as she said this, but Candace's eyes lit up.

"A wedding tea?" she repeated. "What's that?"

Jan explained her hopes for the wedding tea: the idea that it would take the place of the rehearsal dinner, and also give guests a flavor of what she and Elaine had been devoting so much of their lives to over the past few years. That it would be more leisurely and less boisterous than a dinner—and also get both adults and kids home at a reasonable hour the night before the wedding.

"I love this idea," Candace said. "And I've never heard anything like it. I think it might make a good article. Would you be willing to let me come to the tearoom to do coverage on the story?"

At her question, Jan felt the pressure in her chest tighten a bit. With everything else she was trying to do, was now really the moment to add another thing to the mix? Especially when that other thing was a reporter who would be reporting on her and her business not at a moment she would have naturally chosen to showcase it, but at a moment when she was already feeling stressed and vulnerable?

But at the same time, healthy pride swelled in her chest, knocking away some of the worry. It was gratifying to hear that Candace thought her idea for the wedding tea was a good one, not a crazy one. And any press that Tea for Two could get was good for the business.

"Of course," Jan said.

"This will be a wonderful local color story," Candace declared, hunting through her calendar to find a time. "Will that time work for you?"

Jan nodded and noted it in her own daybook—although there was hardly any chance she would forget. More likely, she'd have to stop herself from thinking about the upcoming visit until Candace actually showed up.

"And I had a question for you," Jan said.

"Oh?" Candace shifted her computer screen to the side. "What's that?"

"Well, Elaine and I have been loving *The Crooked Lake Mystery* you've been printing for the past few weeks," Jan began.

Was it her imagination, or did a flash of pleasure and pride light up Candace's eyes? Whatever it was, Candace quickly covered it with a polite smile.

"I'm so glad to hear that," she said.

"I suspect I'm not the only person who's told you that," Jan said.

But now Candace, who had been so open and friendly just a moment before, would hardly meet her eyes at all. "It has been a surprisingly popular feature."

"I hope a pleasant surprise," Jan said.

Candace nodded, almost curtly. Maybe working with River White for all those years had started to rub off on her, Jan thought.

"And we're a little curious," Jan tried, in hopes of working her way slowly up to the point.

But at the mention of the word curious, Candace's eyes turned wary.

When she didn't say anything, Jan was forced to plunge on. "About the author," she said. "We love that story so much, we'd love to read more. But we just looked the name up on the Internet and couldn't find anything else by that name."

Candace's expression turned from wary to something that looked quite a bit like displeased.

Suddenly, Jan felt a wave of worry. In all her years of knowing Candace, she'd never asked her about any of her other work beyond the paper, or asked to read more based on anything Candace had written. Had she inadvertently insulted Candace by lavishing so much praise on this other writer? Candace had never seemed like the jealous type to her before.

But, Jan knew from her own passionate feelings about baking, it was hard to predict how people were going to react when you stepped onto the delicate footing of how they felt about their creative projects.

"I couldn't tell you who wrote that story," Candace said. "For that, you'd have to see River."

Jan was never eager to talk with River, but she was eager to get out of this conversation with Candace. "Is he in today?" she asked.

As soon as Candace nodded, Jan half-regretted asking. "Right back there," Candace said. "In his office."

Somewhat reluctantly, Jan rose.

"Well, thank you," she said. "I'll see you when you come to the tearoom for the article."

At this, Candace's expression seemed to soften. "See you then," she said.

Jan looked longingly back up at the front door, where she knew she could make a quick escape and hear a friendly word from Cookie on the way out, rather than confronting River White in his "office," which was really more like a nook in the back of the newsroom.

But instead, she turned and headed toward the low partition wall that separated River's desk from the rest of the office.

When she reached it, River looked up. He clearly recognized her, and just as clearly wasn't totally thrilled to see her.

"Can I help you?" he asked.

CHAPTER SEVEN

Sometimes in the past, River's lack of filter had made Jan feel as if she must have said or done the wrong thing.

But this time, she knew she hadn't done anything wrong. She was a paying customer of his paper, who had come in on legitimate business with a genuine question about something he printed. Answering her was just part of his job description.

Sweetly, Jan sat down in the seat beside his desk, to make it plain that she had no intention of going anywhere until she got what she had come for—which, at the bare minimum, was an answer to her questions.

"I've just been talking with Candace," she said. "She told me you were the one to answer a question I had."

"What's that?" River asked.

"Well, Elaine and I have been enjoying *The Crooked Lake Mystery* serial you've been running this holiday season," Jan said.

At this, River shook his head, as if he thought having a hit series of articles was a big annoyance—perhaps because the story was fiction and not the serious reporting he was always trying to do. "You and every other subscriber we've got anywhere in the Chickadee Lake area."

"I can imagine it's popular," Jan said. "The writing is excellent."

River pursed his lips. It seemed he couldn't bring himself to disagree with that, at least.

"And now that it's over, we were wondering where we could read more," Jan said. "Can you tell me anything else at all about the author?"

"No," River said simply.

Jan had to admit that his directness was effective. He had given her almost nothing to go on to continue the conversation, not even a reason to argue with.

"Do you mind telling me why?" Jan asked. "Is it some kind of secret?"

"I can't tell you," River repeated.

Jan pressed her lips together. "I just can't understand what harm it would do anyone for you to let us know how to find out more about the author," she said. "Even if they want to guard their privacy, don't they want people to read their writing? They must, if they've allowed this story to be published. And by its quality, I can't imagine there isn't more out there."

River just looked at her.

As Jan's eyes darted around his desk, in search of some idea, any idea, they landed on a copy of the latest edition, folded up on top of a stack of notebooks and stray paper.

An inspiration formed in her mind. Plenty of people had obviously been pestering him about the identity of the author, which he clearly wasn't eager to divulge. And all those encounters had apparently given him some good practice keeping his mouth shut on the topic.

But, she thought to herself, *I bet nobody else has asked him about this.*

"If that's all, I'm afraid I can't help you any further," River said, reaching to retrieve the copy of the paper.

Gently but firmly, Jan held on to it.

"Actually," she said, "there was one other thing."

"What was that?" River asked, in a tone that made it abundantly clear he had very little interest in helping her with whatever "that" turned out to be.

Jan opened the paper, flipped to the page featuring *The Crooked Lake Mystery* installment and folded it back so that she could lay it neatly on River's desk.

"Yes, I've seen this edition," River said. "Probably at least as many times as anyone alive. Our senior editor's been laid up with surgery since Thanksgiving, so this time around, I'm the one who put it to bed."

"But have you seen this?" Jan asked.

She ran her finger down the left-hand margin of the story, until it came to the words she had discovered there earlier that morning.

For the first time, she seemed to have River's attention. But now, instead of annoyed, his expression had changed into something else. Was it anger? Fear? A bit of both?

"Meet," she read. *"Sea Pine Park. Five."*

As she read, River's eyes bulged out. She couldn't tell if his reaction was due to the fact that he'd never seen it himself, despite all his claims about knowing the paper better than anyone else—or if his emotions came from the fact that he had seen it and hoped no one else had.

"It's a message," she said.

River leaned back in his chair, pushing the paper out of the way with a dismissive air.

"Now, I don't know that we could go so far as to say that," he said.

"What would you say, then?" Jan asked, being careful to give him a smile as she spoke.

"I've seen thousands and thousands of newspaper columns," River said. "It might be more like hundreds of thousands. Or even millions. All those columns, all those letters, jumbled together randomly. Every now and then, I'm sure something is going to look like a message to *someone*."

The emphasis he put on *someone* made it very clear what he thought of anyone who went around believing they'd discovered messages hidden in the newspaper columns of local papers.

"Well, if you've seen so many newspaper columns, then you must have seen a few of these yourself," Jan said. "Which ones have you seen?"

"I don't make a habit of reading my papers for secret codes. So I really couldn't say."

"If they're common though," Jan persisted, "then I guess we could expect to find some other words that randomly show up in any paper. Like this one."

She began to run her fingers down the left-hand column of the opposite page. "Oh, look," she said. "Here's one. *Ten. Y, N, J, H, T, C, O, A, G,*" she continued, reading out the random letters that poured down the column, along the page. "And here's another. *Sat. P, J, C, E, E, Y, S, S, D, H, K, G*...nope. No others in this column."

She scanned down the next column and the one after that, finding *it, at,* and *yin,* but nothing else.

"None of these words are longer than three letters," she said. "And none of them appear back to back. And none of them seem to spell anything that looks like a message."

She turned back to the first page containing *The Crooked Lake Mystery,* where the message she'd pointed out still stood out clearly on the left-hand side.

"This message is four words long. Five, if you count the *OC* for o'clock. Obviously, I'm no expert on random gatherings of words in newspapers, but just based on the quick experiment we've done here together today, I'd say I find it quite unusual."

River had retreated to his earlier tactic of simply not answering, but she could tell from the way his jaw was working that he was operating under some kind of strong emotion.

"Would you say you find it unusual?" Jan asked. "Even a little bit?"

River took a deep breath and seemed to come to some conclusion deep within himself. He leaned forward. "Have you heard of the *Bible Code,* Ms. Blake?" he asked.

Jan tilted her head to indicate she had. But she hadn't paid much attention to it.

"It was quite a popular book, about twenty years ago," River went on. "I was a high school reporter then, just starting out. Which meant I was required to write a review of it, so I became quite intimately acquainted with the book. And with some of its primary critics."

There was nothing River liked better than holding forth on a topic on which he believed himself to be an expert. And Jan could see life begin to come into his expression as he warmed to his subject.

"If you read the book on its own, it seems quite compelling," he said. "Using those old techniques, you can cull all kinds of things that sound like messages, especially from a book such as the Bible, which doesn't have vowels in much of the original Hebrew. That means that anyone looking for a code gets to put in their own vowels. *S-T,* for instance. That could read *sit, sat, sot,* or *set,* depending on what vowel a would-be code-hunter chooses to insert. And reading text not just horizontally but vertically introduces all kinds of interesting possibilities."

"Exactly," Jan said.

River smiled with satisfaction. "The problem, Ms. Blake," he said, "is that you can find all those same possibilities if you apply the same rationale to *The Count of Monte Cristo.* Or *On the Origin of Species.* Or the New York City phone book. Twenty years ago," he added. "Back when they still printed it."

Jan leaned back in her chair with a feeling that she was being had. She looked back at the copy of the *Penzance Courier* on the desk. "This message has its vowels included," she said. "It's much less open to interpretation."

River sighed. "Well, then what do you think it means?"

"I don't know," Jan said. "It looks as though it's setting up some kind of meeting. At the park."

"Yes, yes. At five o'clock. But when?"

Jan looked back at him. He had her there.

"I'm sorry," River said. "But if there is a code here, whoever wrote it doesn't strike me as very intelligent. They arrange a time, but not a date."

"Maybe the date is in another paper," Jan said.

"I assume you've done this"—River paused as if searching for the word—"*sleuthing* through all the chapters of the serial?"

Jan nodded. Just like with everything else, she'd been conscientious in this. Once the first stray word had caught her eye, she'd combed back through all the chapters she'd already read, and all the ones that followed, several times.

"But you didn't find any reference to a date?"

Jan shook her head.

"And this is, as I'm sure you've noticed, the final episode in the series."

Jan nodded, but also lifted her chin. "It could be in another paper," she said. "In one of the next issues."

At this, River grinned with something that might even have been admiration.

"Even I can't tell you exactly what's going to be in our next issues," he said. "Because the news hasn't happened yet."

"Furthermore," he added, gaining the glint again of a man warming to his topic, "it would be nearly impossible for anyone in this office to put a code in the paper, even if we wanted to."

He leaned back in his chair, looking pleased.

"Well, thank you for your time," Jan said, rising.

CHAPTER EIGHT

"That sounds great, honey," Elaine said. "You'll get here just in time."

"Fingers crossed," her son, Jared, said at the other end of the line. In the background, she could hear the rumble of the road, where he was calling from. He and Corrine had just gotten the kids in the car and were in the first hours of their journey from Ohio to spend Christmas with Elaine. But, Elaine noticed, she didn't hear the sounds of Lucy and Micah, her grandchildren, bickering in the background. That was a good sign, at least for now.

"Thanks for making the drive, honey," Elaine said.

"Of course, Mom."

"I know it's not a simple thing to take kids on a trip that long," Elaine said.

"How do you know that?" Jared joked. "Did you have pesky kids of your own?"

Elaine smiled. "Sometimes they grow up all right."

"That's what I'm hoping," Jared said. "Okay, better go."

"Love you," Elaine said.

As she hung up the phone, she caught sight through the window of Earl Grey. He was an outdoor cat, and she knew he was plenty warm with his fur coat, but maybe he was looking for company.

And she could use some company herself.

When she went out to his shelter on the screened-in back porch, Earl Grey jumped neatly from the roof of the winter shelter and stood on his back legs to bump his grey head against her hand, begging for a caress.

Elaine scratched his ears gratefully.

She had thought she would feel better once she got back home and talked to Jan, that all her worries about Nathan would recede into the distance, or come into perspective.

I'm going to see him tonight, she had told herself as she'd made a pot of one of her favorite new teas, a mint rose, as a tactic to distract herself. *I'll ask him about everything then. I'm sure there's some kind of explanation. And until then, I just won't think about it.*

It was probably good advice, but it was a lot easier said than done.

In fact, when she'd curled up in a chair in the sitting room with her tea, intending to give herself a little break before she dived back into the rest of her day, she couldn't stop thinking about it. The more she tried not to think about Nathan and the woman, the more her mind tugged in that direction, just like a kid or a dog who got curious about something at the exact moment you told them it was off limits.

Then another thought popped into her head: it wasn't just that she was upset over seeing another woman kiss Nathan—and him accept her kiss. It was much deeper than that.

Her heart twinged in her chest as she came face-to-face with what was really bothering her: the nagging thought that, if there wasn't a good explanation, she might have to let go of her relationship with Nathan.

She'd thought of this, of course, before, but in a very abstract way. If they didn't get married, she'd thought, one day they'd have to go their separate ways. But that was always long, long in the future—not the suddenly possible reality it now seemed to be.

And she'd thought about it on days when she was feeling especially independent, or when it had started to feel like a little bit of a hassle to make time for Nathan: a little thrill of happiness over her freedom and the fact that she wasn't tied down the way she had been when she was married and had to share everything with someone else whether she wanted to or not. It wasn't that Elaine was secretive, or that she didn't want to share things with Nathan. One of her favorite parts about their relationship was sharing the events of their days and weeks, listening to his perspective on her life, and feeling grateful for the way he always seemed to want to know what she thought about the things that had been going on in his world, and what he should do about them. Not every man was like that, but Nathan said he wanted a true partnership, and he had a way of proving it—by treating her as a partner.

But now, the idea of losing him as part of her life gave her no feeling of freedom at all. In fact, it hurt—and once she let it in, it completely took over her thoughts.

But it didn't take them over the way she might have expected.

Elaine was a hardheaded woman, in the best sense of the word. She had never been afraid to look at a situation head-on, no matter how tough it was. And it was an attitude that had served her well all her life as she'd had to confront new situation after new situation as she and Ben had moved all around the world.

In this case, she expected to have to take a good hard look at what she would lose if she were to lose Nathan: his perspective, his help around the tearoom, his penchant for choosing new places to visit that he thought she might like, his hopeful attitude about the future that always helped her when her own realism started to get her down. And all of his tenderness: the way he always wanted to protect her, even though she had been taking care of herself for so long, the way he always reached for her hand whenever they walked anyplace together, and the kisses that still made her heart flutter, long after the first one they'd shared.

But to her surprise, instead of thinking about what she stood to lose, her mind wandered off. Suddenly, she found herself thinking about what it would be like to be married to Nathan. In her mind's eye, she saw him coming through the door after a day spent out, dropping his coat on a kitchen chair, then gathering her up to give her a kiss. She saw the two of them reading companionably in the evening, with the lights of their home warm and cozy despite the darkness beyond the windows. She pictured him sneaking a bite of something as she cooked, then laughing as she swatted him away.

As these thoughts flowed through Elaine's mind, her heart swelled with hope—and love.

So when her mind flashed back on the image of him kissing the other woman, it was simply too much.

Not even sure where she was going, she'd stood and found herself downstairs and wandering out to the little hutch they'd created for Earl Grey, pulling her sweater around herself against the cold.

The sweet cat was meowing for her full attention, apparently able to tell that she was in no state to be left alone.

But if she didn't want to waste the whole day in fruitless circles, she needed to find something else to occupy her mind. Something more interesting than the past day's receipts.

Like all the strange details in *The Crooked Lake Mystery,* that seemed to track so closely with her own personal history.

As Earl Grey slipped through her ankles, then back again, reluctant to leave her alone, Elaine gave him one last good scratch on his head, then went inside and up to the sitting room, grabbed her laptop, and settled back down again with her tea.

She and Jan had already discovered that previous issues of *The Crooked Lake Mystery* appeared on the paper's website around the same time they were printed. And now she was glad to discover that the final episode was posted already, along with the previous ones, all the way back to the first chapter.

"Well," Elaine said to herself. "Let's see how this looks if we start from the beginning."

Starting with the first line of the entire story, she began to skim through each installment, paragraph by paragraph, looking for anything that jogged her memory or jumped out anew as possibly referring to her, and jotting it down when she did.

As she scanned, from time to time she glanced at the line of letters that dropped down the left-hand column of the page, checking for any further "secret messages" like the ones Jan thought she had found. Elaine could tell that the formatting hadn't been retained from the printed newspaper version. In fact, the layout online was much more similar to the page of a book than a newspaper, with one large single column that expanded or contracted depending on how large she had set her web browser.

She did catch a few words here and there: *fin, at, on.* But nothing, she had to admit, as lengthy, or as cogent, as the messages that Jan believed she had uncovered. Maybe Jan was on to something, after all, she thought.

But mostly, she concentrated on any of the details she could find about the Laney character and, secondarily, Jon, who she suspected was also based on Jim Biggers.

The more she looked at the Jon character, the more he seemed to be closely linked to Jim. And the more it seemed that the author had known him quite a bit better than Elaine ever had. The Jon character played football—the offensive tackle position—just as Jim had. Elaine had only ever had a hint that Jim might struggle with reading, but the author either knew or had dreamed up a whole backstory about his struggles to take in information from the page, even though he had a quick and clever mind. Was it possible that he had been dyslexic, at a time when that was rarely diagnosed?

But at least Elaine had had a glimpse of those struggles of Jim's herself. Other details the author had included about Jon, if Jon really had anything to do with the real-life Jim, suggested that Jim had been dealing with a lot more than Elaine had ever dreamed of when she'd spent the few breezy weeks dating him.

In the story, Jon's mother was quite sick, and another reason he struggled in school was that he was always trying to balance his football practice, his friends, and his classes with the enormous amount of time he also spent caring for his mom.

But he did have a secret outlet, just for himself. Around his neighborhood, he'd become known as something of an amateur veterinarian. From the time he was a boy, apparently, when he'd found a wounded sparrow flapping around under the oak tree in his backyard and nursed it back to health, he'd always had a knack for helping animals, wild or tame, recover from sickness or injuries. So more often than not, according to *The Crooked Lake Mystery,* the Jon character also had some quiet moments to himself, nursing a baby raccoon with an eye dropper, or replenishing the fresh seed in the glass box of a recovering bird. Maybe, the story seemed to suggest, he found these moments meaningful because he actually was able to help the wounded animals back to health, while his mother's condition, which was chronic, never really improved by much, no matter what he did.

Were these stories true details from Jim's life? Elaine felt slightly embarrassed to realize she didn't know. Of course, she hadn't dated Jim for very long—no more than a month or two, if that. But she couldn't say for sure what his mother looked like, whether she was sickly or not—even what his father did.

And she couldn't think of any hobby of Jim's besides his life at the high school and the few dates they'd gone on together, which were just like any date, really: a trip to the movies, grabbing a few scoops of ice cream, watching the sun go down over Chickadee Lake.

Had she really never bothered to ask even those simple questions about him? Or had Jim's life been so much more complicated than she realized that he had done his best to hide the true details of it from her?

Elaine felt a pang of embarrassment, but even more deeply a kind of sorrow. Had she really been so incurious about someone she'd known, even that well? What other questions had it never occurred to her to ask about other people in her life? Of course, they were all kids in those days, all worried about fitting in and learning how to get along in the world themselves. But what had she missed along the way? And was she still missing similar things in her life now?

Those questions, however, were pushed aside by the feeling of unease that grew in her as she went back through the story with a laser-focus on the character of Laney. She had half-hoped that on a second read her fears would dissipate—she'd discover that Laney was actually quite different from her, or that the details weren't nearly as on-the-nose to her own life as she'd thought at first blush.

But instead, the opposite happened. The reason she hadn't noticed the character of Laney much until the final pages was that she hadn't been foregrounded as an important character. This was a great move on the part of the writer, who managed to keep Laney present but not obtrusive, so that it was a genuine surprise even to readers as sophisticated and sharp-eyed as Jan and Elaine when the identity of the murderer was revealed.

But that meant that only a detail or two was given about Laney every time she appeared. And as Elaine read through those descriptions, she realized that not just some of them, but *all* of them applied to her. Some of them were tweaked slightly, such as the detail Bianca had noticed, where the Laney character added lace to her jacket, instead of rickrack. But some of them were dead on. The Laney character had a habit of saying "Good grief!" which had been one of her favorite expressions around the time she was sixteen. She also had a penchant for baby blue, which Elaine would have dressed in from head to toe if her budget had allowed an entire overhaul of her wardrobe at that age.

They were all small enough details that they hadn't caught Elaine's eye until the more personal ones began to stack up at the end. And taken alone, many of them were details that could have applied to any number of girls in high school in this area at the time—or in high schools around the country, for that matter.

But taken together, they added up to a description of only one person Elaine could name: herself.

As she looked over the list she'd made, then looked it over again, trying to find even one detail about the Laney character that she could definitively say had nothing to do with her, and failing, Jan walked in.

She took one look at Elaine's face and seemed to realize that something wasn't quite right.

"Hey," she said, putting her purse down. "How are you doing?"

What felt like dozens of ideas swirled through Elaine's head: the details of the newspaper story, even Jan's scones. But at her cousin's question, one thing rose clearly through all of them: the strange woman she had seen kissing Nathan.

"I saw something that bothered me," she said.

"Oh?" Jan settled down on a nearby chair with a listening expression.

"I saw Nathan at the Odyssey," Elaine said. "With a woman." In her head, the words had felt weighty and scary, but when she spoke them out loud, they didn't sound so bad. Of course, she hadn't told the whole story yet. Which perhaps was why Jan didn't seem very rattled by the news herself.

"Who was it? Did you talk to them?"

"No," Elaine said. "But I saw her kiss him."

This did get Jan's attention. But she still didn't seem to feel the hurt Elaine felt, or the outrage Elaine might expect Jan to have, taking her side. Instead, Jan's eyebrows just jumped slightly.

"That sounds strange," she said.

Elaine nodded. "It felt...strange. I'd never seen the woman before."

"What did Nathan do when she kissed him?" Jan asked.

"I didn't see," Elaine said. "I realized they could see me, so I ducked behind a newspaper."

"Well, have you asked him about it?"

It was such a sensible question that Elaine suddenly felt foolish for not just having the rational conversation that Jan clearly expected her to have with Nathan about the whole thing. "No," she said. "Nathan's been a little hard to get in touch with." She couldn't quite bring herself to articulate her big fear: that he had been hard to get in touch with because he was spending time with this other woman.

"I can't say I'd want to see something like that myself," Jan said. "But don't let your imagination run away with you. Not before you talk with him."

Elaine looked up, feeling a faint tinge of hope. "Speaking of the newspaper," she said, "how did it go?"

If Jan had learned anything about the identity of the writer, maybe they could put all the questions that were swirling around in her head to rest at last. Maybe it could have even been a friend of theirs who had written the story, as some kind of misguided joke.

But Jan just shook her head. "Nothing. I couldn't get Candace or River to tell me anything about the author."

Elaine realized that her face must have fallen, because Jan reached over and gave her shoulder a squeeze.

"Don't worry," she said. "It's not such a big deal." She looked down at the list in Elaine's lap. "What's all this?"

Briefly, Elaine walked Jan through the list. When she got to the end, Jan reached for it. "Do you mind?" she asked.

"Sure," Elaine said, releasing it.

As Jan scanned through the items, her brow furrowed.

"You know...," she began.

"What?" Elaine asked.

"Something strikes me about this list," Jan said, looking up. "It's full of details about you. Or at least," she corrected herself, "details that are like the details of your life."

Elaine nodded.

"But nothing about your life after high school. None of your travels, Germany, Italy, Hawaii, Japan, Belgium. Nothing about Ben, or Sasha or Jared. Nothing about the tearoom."

"That's true," Elaine said, the gears in her mind starting to turn.

"If this author really did know you, I'd say they haven't been in touch with you for quite some time."

"Not since high school," Elaine said.

Jan nodded. "Anyway, I need to get back downstairs. With all that baking this morning, I didn't manage to make any biscuits or cookies. And it's quite possible," she said, "that we'll have a guest today who'd like to try something other than a scone."

Elaine smiled as Jan turned to go.

But when she was left alone in the room again, her heart did an unsteady little flip.

Thinking back on high school always made her think about everything that had happened since then, both what she'd gained and what had been lost. But before now, her memories of high school itself had basically been good ones.

Now, however, she wondered how much she had missed. What had she not known about Jim? About anyone else? Had someone disliked her and she'd never realized it? And if so, why was the story just surfacing in the paper, all these decades later?

CHAPTER NINE

At first, Jan couldn't believe her eyes.

She'd seen the face of the woman standing in the entryway of Tea for Two hundreds of times, so often that she would recognize her anywhere: the aquiline nose, the arch of her brows, the auburn hair that fell in improbably perfect waves over her shoulders, the face that seemed ageless, despite all the years that had passed since Jan first saw her.

Now, of course, she looked slightly different: her high cheekbones chapped red by the nip of the winter air outside, her hair slightly tousled, and its color set off by a gigantic teal scarf, which appeared to be composed of so many yards of soft wool that it could be used to help warm a small army in a pinch, or even serve as a tent, if it came to that.

Her expression was different than Jan had ever seen before as well: in place of the knowing smile Jan was used to was an air of wonder and curiosity, and perhaps even delight, as she looked around at all the treasures Jan and Elaine had tucked away here and there to welcome visitors to the Tea for Two entry.

But despite the fact that Jan's mind registered her with all the familiarity of an old friend, Jan had never actually seen the woman before in real life, other than on the dust jacket of one of her and Elaine's favorite mystery series.

"Vanessa van Dyke," Jan breathed, before she realized she was speaking out loud.

As soon as she did, she felt a wave of embarrassment.

It wasn't that she couldn't hold her own around an accomplished guest. She and Elaine had hosted their share of VIPs at Tea for Two—and perhaps even more guests who *thought* of themselves as VIPs. Jan had never been intimidated by them. In fact, she always felt a bit of sympathy for what it must be like to move through the world with everyone always thinking they knew something about you, just because they happened to know your name.

Which was why she winced now.

She'd never met Vanessa van Dyke before. If she'd been just a little bit less of a fan, she might not have blurted out her name. And now that she had, she hoped that it hadn't made Vanessa uncomfortable. Jan wanted her to know that she'd be treated just like anybody else at Tea for Two and that nobody would invade her privacy—including Jan.

But Vanessa just gave her a big grin and stuck out her hand. "Guilty," she said. "And you are?"

Relieved, Jan took Vanessa's hand, still chilly from her journey to the tearoom, and shook it. "I'm Jan," she said. "And a big fan of yours. As I guess you can see."

But before she could say anything else, someone else slipped through the front door, directly behind Vanessa.

Jan's smile faded slightly when she recognized who it was.

"Well, this is it," Macy Atherton said, smacking her hands together to bring some warmth back into them. She looked around the entryway with a critical eye. "Such as it is."

"It's lovely," Vanessa said.

"She wanted to see the tearoom," Macy said to Jan, in a tone that was both confiding and slightly exasperated, as if she couldn't understand why in the world anyone would want to do such a thing.

"Would you like to sit down?" Jan asked.

"Could we?" Vanessa asked. "That sounds just wonderful."

"I'm sure you've been to better tearooms than this," Macy said, trailing after Vanessa as Vanessa followed Jan to a table. As they were seated, Macy gave Jan a significant look. "Vanessa's an author. A very successful one. With over a dozen best sellers on the *New York Times* list."

"Oh my goodness," Vanessa said, looking slightly mortified, while at the same time also looking slightly pleased.

"She's staying with me at Green Glade." Macy leaned back in her chair as if she'd just played a winning hand at cards.

"Now, tell me," Vanessa said, seemingly trying to distract Macy from her line of conversation. "Is there something I just *must* try here?"

As she did, Elaine came in the door from the kitchen and stopped dead in her tracks.

"Vanessa van Dyke!" she exclaimed.

Around the tearoom, the heads of the other patrons started to turn.

Instantly, Elaine collected herself and walked over to the table with the large plate of scones she'd collected in the kitchen. Her plan, she had told Jan, was to display some of the wares that Jan had baked, in hopes that they would sell more quickly if the mouthwatering treats were displayed for every patron to see, rather than just listed as items on the menu or mentioned as specials by their servers.

With Vanessa, at least, her plan worked.

"What in the world are these?" she asked, her eyes widening.

"Scones," Macy said shortly. "You've seen scones before."

"But not like these," Vanessa said. "Look at this frosting, the tiny gridwork. I've never seen anything like it." Her brow furrowed as she spoke. "Except…on cross-stitch. Look at these tiny hearts! I don't know that I've ever seen anything so darling."

Beside Elaine, Jan beamed.

"Now tell me," Vanessa leaned forward, "what bakery do you work with? Are these made here in town?"

"They're made here at Tea for Two," Elaine said, setting a scone down on Vanessa's empty plate and, after the slightest hesitation, one for Macy as well. "And you've already met the baker."

She tilted her head to indicate Jan.

Vanessa took a bite of her scone and closed her eyes, a picture of bliss. "You bake these wonderful things?" she asked Jan.

Jan nodded, trying to suppress the wide grin that threatened to take over her whole face.

On the other side of the table, Macy glanced at Vanessa with eagerness, not wanting to miss out on the treat if it really was so magical, but at the same time suspicious that nothing could actually be as magical as Vanessa seemed to think the scone was—especially not something at Tea for Two. She took a bite of her own scone.

"It's just strawberry glaze," she announced, but then paused uncertainly. "Isn't it?"

"But *what* strawberry glaze!" Vanessa enthused. "I don't think I've had anything like it. Not at the highest tea in England."

"Vanessa has had tea all over the world," Macy took the opportunity to announce. "Moscow, London, Paris, New York City..."

"What brings you to Lancaster?" Jan asked.

"And so close to Christmas," Elaine said. "Do you have friends in town?"

For the first time, Vanessa's wide smile flickered.

"She's staying for a week," Macy said proudly. "Until after Christmas."

Jan's eyes widened in surprise. "That's a long visit for over the holidays."

By now, Vanessa had recovered herself. She waved her hand airily. "Oh," she said, "when you've been as many places as I have, you start to realize that what you really want around the holidays is something that feels like home."

"Did you grow up in a town like Lancaster?" Jan asked.

Vanessa shook her head. "No, actually," she said. "I grew up in Los Angeles. My mother had dreams of being a movie star."

"Well," Jan said, "I always thought you could be a movie star, if being a writer didn't work out for you. Your author picture is so striking."

"And accurate, apparently." Vanessa laughed. "I do get recognized quite often."

"I wouldn't think a small town would feel like home, then," Elaine said.

"To be honest," Vanessa said, "I can't say Los Angeles ever felt like home to me, even when I was growing up there. My mother was from a small town, so I guess maybe I inherited the idea of small town as home from her and all her stories of the marvels of a small-town Christmas. With real snow on the ground," she added, and laughed. "Like you have here."

"Except it's not like in a postcard," Macy said. "If it's on the ground, you actually have to walk through it."

"That's true." Vanessa looked ruefully down at her boots. "But even that seems like an adventure to me. At least so far. And I expect the whole town will be an adventure. I'm going to explore everything."

"That won't take you long," Macy half-snorted.

"Oh, I'll take my time with it," Vanessa promised. "And I think some places I'll really want to get to know. Like this one," she said, smiling up at Jan and Elaine.

"But Lancaster, though," Elaine said. "I mean, I can tell you why *I* think it's the greatest little town in the world. But I'm so curious why you would choose it. What caught your eye, if you'd never been here before?"

For the first time in the conversation, the shadow of a frown crossed Vanessa's face. But it was so brief that Jan wasn't sure she had even seen it.

"You know," Vanessa said, with an even brighter smile, "I think it might have been the lake. I had explored a handful of little towns with high-rated independent inns, like Macy's..."

Macy beamed.

"...but I think what really made Lancaster stand out was the lake. I mean, Chickadee Lake," she said. "I don't know if I could have named that better myself."

Still preening in the glow of the compliment she'd received from Vanessa, Macy finally decided to give a rare one of her own. "And the tearoom," she said. "You mentioned that to me as soon as you checked in."

"Did I?" Vanessa asked. "Oh yes, I guess I did."

"You said you'd seen it online," Macy insisted. "It was one of the first things you asked. And you wanted to know how to get here from Green Glade. I was worried it might not live up to everything you'd imagined—"

Vanessa seemed to realize how insulting Macy could be, even if Macy didn't. She broke in before Macy could get too much further. "Oh, I imagine all kinds of things," she said. "Good and bad. But this has exceeded my highest hopes."

"How in the world did you find us online?" Jan asked.

"I'm not sure," Vanessa said. "I guess just rabbit trail to rabbit trail. I'm a bit like Alice, I'm afraid."

"Including a love for tea," Elaine joked.

"Exactly," Vanessa said, with something like relief. She looked down at the menus that Jan had placed in their hands as they sat down. "Now, what shall we have? I'm trying to decide between this orange rooibos and this mint rose."

"The mint rose is lovely," Elaine said. "I was just sampling some of it earlier today."

"But there's also this hand-crafted chamomile," Vanessa said. "That's always been my favorite. It's one of the ways I size up a tearoom, if you know what I mean. How they do a simple chamomile."

"I could get the rooibos, if you want to get the chamomile," Macy suggested, with what seemed to Jan like uncharacteristic helpfulness. Macy had *some* skills in customer service, Jan knew, even if she didn't use them much when she was a customer herself. At least not at Tea for Two.

"That sounds good," Vanessa said, as Jan made a mental note of what they'd need to prep back in the kitchen. "But the mint rose..."

"You could get it next time," Macy suggested.

Surprised, Jan gave her a grateful smile at her assumption that Vanessa van Dyke would ever be repeat business for Tea for Two.

Vanessa pursed her lips and looked up at Jan and Elaine. "Would it be crazy to get three pots? I know we can't possibly drink them all, but I don't think I can bear not to try all three."

"Of course," Jan said, and started to step back and head for the kitchen.

But before she could go, Vanessa raised her hand. "And what are these?" she asked. "It's not just scones—you have actual tea sandwiches?"

"Of course," Elaine said.

Jan looked at her cousin, amused. She wouldn't have thought that it would be Vanessa instead of Macy who would get Elaine's back up, but apparently Elaine was slightly miffed over the idea that Tea for Two would ever serve anything other than a truly proper tea.

"Oh my goodness," Vanessa said, completely ignoring the faint edge to Elaine's tone. "We'll have to have some of those. *Piles* of them, I think. Let's see." She ran her finger down the list in the menu, reading. *"Egg salad. Cucumber. Watercress. And ham."*

"That'll be a lot of sandwich," Macy warned.

Once again, Jan felt grateful that she wasn't the one who had to say it.

"They do give good servings here," Macy went on, almost grudgingly. "Not just a thin slice of bread with some butter wiped on it."

"Then it's a good thing I came hungry," Vanessa said. She laid the menu aside and smiled up at them. "I can't wait to try it all."

CHAPTER TEN

"Vanessa van Dyke," Elaine said to Jan once the tearoom had closed and they were in the kitchen cleaning up. "I never would have guessed she'd set foot in this place."

"Despite all the time we've spent with her," Jan joked.

"That's true," Elaine mused, dunking the third teapot for Vanessa's last order of tea into the soapy water in the sink. "You do spend a great deal of time with an author, in a way, when you read their work. But they don't spend the same kind of time with you."

"Maybe they do," Jan said as she brushed off the crumbs from Vanessa's many plates. "When they sit down to write."

"Could be," Elaine agreed. "But what I still can't get over is that she would ever turn up in Lancaster to begin with."

"You heard her," Jan said. "Not many towns this size have a tearoom like ours. You just need to learn how to take a compliment." She grinned at her cousin.

"Or, maybe Vanessa van Dyke is actually the author of *The Crooked Lake Mystery*. She's been having trouble getting the

Penzance Courier to pay on time, so she came to town herself to make sure she gets her check."

"You figured her out," Jan said, laughing.

But as the laughter between them died away, the cousins locked eyes.

"That story is a lot higher quality than anything I remember the *Penzance Courier* ever printing before," Jan ventured.

"*Much* higher," Elaine added.

"Do you really think…?" Jan began.

"Well, it might explain why a star like Vanessa van Dyke would decide to spend Christmas in Lancaster," Elaine said.

"It would," Jan allowed. "But then we have another mystery."

"What's that?" Elaine asked.

"Why a star like Vanessa van Dyke would publish a story under a pen name at a paper like the *Penzance Courier*," Jan said.

Elaine sighed. "You've got me there. And I'm not convinced she wrote that story, either. I just can't quite believe she's here in Lancaster for no particular reason."

"You know what I can't believe?" Jan asked.

"What's that?"

"I can't believe she ordered the whole menu," Jan said. "I hope she's not planning on a big dinner."

At the mention of dinner, a memory popped in Elaine's head. She looked down at her watch. It was 4:45, but just a few minutes before she'd promised Nathan earlier that week that she'd meet him for dinner.

She was relieved that somehow she'd managed to get through the day, with all of her worries, without jumping to any conclusions. And apparently she'd managed to get engrossed enough in the question of Vanessa van Dyke's visit to Lancaster that she'd even forgotten about her worries for a few pleasant moments.

But now that she remembered her dinner date, she was also grateful the appointment was so soon. Since some time had passed, the fear had drained out of her mind and heart, and her basic trust and love for Nathan had taken their rightful places.

There was some explanation for what she'd seen this morning with the other woman, she thought. And she couldn't wait to get it all settled. And to see him. It had been too long since they connected, and she missed him.

"I've got to go out," she said. "I just remembered. Can you finish the cleanup?" As Elaine asked, a hopeful smile played on her lips.

In answer, Jan gave her a teasing smile of her own. "Just as long as you're not going out to meet up with that bum, Nathan," she joked. "Will I be glad when you finally get over him."

Elaine felt a little pang at the thought of getting over Nathan, even though Jan would never have made the joke if she'd understood what Elaine had been dealing with that day.

But her fondness for him and her hope of getting everything straightened out when she saw him brought a genuine smile to her lips, which she wore even as she slipped out of the kitchen and upstairs to put on a little brighter top and take a look at her hair.

As she got dressed, she even put on a pair of simple vintage earrings. They weren't anything special—she had just picked them up at Sylvia's Closet next door when she had wandered in one day—but it gave her a thrill to feel that she was doing a little something extra to get ready for her date.

The restaurant where they had planned to meet was out of town, on a pretty wooded lot between Lancaster and Penzance.

As Elaine drove there, she began to rehearse in her head what she wanted to say and how to say it. Should she tell him what she had seen and ask about it directly? And if so, should she let him know she trusted him, or just leave her question in the air to hang?

By the time she got to the restaurant, she had decided to begin simply by asking how Nathan's day had been. There was a good chance the answer might emerge naturally from that, she believed.

And if not, she told herself, she would go ahead and ask him about what she'd seen directly. The two of them had never pussyfooted around any conversation. That was one of the things that she enjoyed most about Nathan. She felt she could really be herself around him without worrying too much about having to pick exactly the right word in order to make sure that she was heard. She had never plotted or planned a conversation with him before. And she didn't see any reason to start now.

Whatever was going on, they would work it out together, just as they always had.

Elaine pulled into the parking lot of the restaurant with a feeling of relief. The arch over the door was decorated with calming, tiny white twinkle lights that gave the impression that anyone who went through them might come out on the other side in a kingdom of fairy winter.

Elaine took a deep breath and let it out, hoping that her day really would be transformed as soon as she crossed the threshold. As she took a parking spot, she scanned the lot, looking for Nathan's car.

But as she switched off the ignition, her phone rang.

She smiled as she saw Nathan's photograph flash up on her phone, to indicate the call was from him.

"Hey, stranger," she said. "I just got here."

Normally Nathan would have had a joke to swap back with her, but this time his voice seemed strange—as if he was under some kind of extreme stress, but playing it calm—so calm that he didn't seem calm at all. "Elaine," he said, "I'm so sorry."

"Sorry for what?" she asked, a knot of worry forming in her stomach. Was he really about to make some terrible confession?

"I thought I'd be able to catch you before you got there," Nathan said. "But things"—his voice trailed off as he seemed to search for the words—"got away from me."

"It's no problem if you're running late," Elaine said. "This place is beautiful. I think you're going to love it."

"I'm sorry," Nathan said. "I'm not going to be able to make it at all."

In retrospect, Elaine realized, this is what he had been trying to tell her all along. But it was so out of character for Nathan to cancel a date with her that it hadn't even occurred to her that that was what he might be doing.

"Are you all right?" she asked.

"I'm fine." Was it her imagination, or did he sound a bit short with her, even impatient? "Don't worry about me."

"Nathan," Elaine said, "what's going on? I had something I wanted to ask you, if you just have—"

In the background, she could hear voices. Was there a man there, or a woman? Where was he calling from, if he wasn't alone?

"I don't have time to explain right now," Nathan said. "But I'll call you later."

"Nathan—"

"Talk to you soon," Nathan said. "Good night."

And then, without waiting for her to answer, he broke their connection.

CHAPTER ELEVEN

What's all this?" Bob asked when he walked into the kitchen of Tea for Two the next morning, to find Jan surrounded by what seemed to be reams of newspaper, spread all over the kitchen counters.

Jan looked up, delighted to see him. He came over and gave her a kiss, then another on the cheek for good measure.

"Let me guess," Bob said. "You're on the hunt for some spectacular scone ingredient. The great Maine snark-berry, with a flavor like nothing else in the known world. But before you can bake it into one of your creations, you have to track down the identity of the last known living snark-grower, an inveterate hermit who hasn't been known to speak to another living soul for the last two decades. Except for his niece, Angelica, whose whereabouts you are trying to locate right now."

"Not quite," Jan said, smiling.

But as she opened her mouth to tell him what she was really doing, she paused, bemused. The story she was about to tell him sounded even crazier when she thought about saying it out loud than the crazy story he had just teased her with.

Maybe River was right after all, and everything she thought she had found in the paper was just coincidence.

Her shoulders slumped slightly at the thought.

Bob put his arm around her and peered down at the paper.

"Hey, none of this," he said. "I didn't mean to discourage you from your search. What are you looking for? You just let me know, I'll be your deputy. There's no way we won't find it together."

"Well," Jan said, "have you been reading that Crooked Lake mystery? In the *Penzance Courier*?"

Bob nodded enthusiastically. "You know, I don't always go in for fiction books," he said. "But I happened to start a chapter of that one day a while after they started running it, just because it caught my eye in the paper. And I'll tell you what, I couldn't get enough. I kept reading after that. And then when I really got into it, I dug up a few copies from my recycling bin, to read the chapters I'd missed, in case there were any good clues in them. I can't believe Laney did it. My money was on the English teacher."

"Me too!" Jan said, her eyes lighting up.

"You know what? It seems you and I kind of think alike. Maybe you should let me take you out one of these days."

Jan grinned. "We'll see about that," she said.

Bob looked down at the papers. "Looks as though you've got an interest in *The Crooked Lake Mystery* too," he said. "Going back through it one more time, just to make sure it all adds up?"

Jan decided not to mention the questions Elaine had about the Laney character to him. Even describing how all the details fit Elaine felt like a violation of her privacy, because some of them were so personal. Realizing this, Jan felt she had a better sense of why Elaine was so upset. If Jan hesitated to even share them with Bob, what must it feel like to Elaine to know they were all out there in the paper for anyone to see? And to know that some people, like Bianca, had already recognized some of them?

But she couldn't put him off indefinitely. So she might as well come out with it, she decided. It wouldn't be the craziest thing she'd ever told him. And somehow, he still wanted to marry her.

"I think there's a code in the paper," Jan said. "So I'm looking for more."

"A code?" Bob asked.

Quickly, Jan flipped from paper to paper, showing Bob the strings of words she'd discovered hiding down the left-hand column of *The Crooked Lake Mystery* chapters. Bob was polite, but only polite, until she started to show him the work she had been doing that morning, looking for other words that appeared at random anywhere else in the paper's text.

The thing was, there weren't any. At least not any to speak of. Just two and three letters here and there, but not anything that ever added up to a four- or five-letter word. "That's remarkable," Bob said, flipping between the pages of the final installment and the rest of the paper, which was full of announcements about Christmas services and advertisements for Christmas concerts. "And there's something else," he said.

"What?" Jan asked.

"Not only are there no four- or five-letter words appearing at random," Bob said. "But you never see two real words appear one after the other, except for in *The Crooked Lake Mystery* text."

"That's right!" Jan said, feeling vindicated.

"And here you've got"—Bob leaned in to count—"three, four, five..." He looked up, his eyes full of lively interest. "I think you're on to something here. But who in the world would be putting a code in the local newspaper?"

"And it's not in a classified ad, where a customer pays for the type," Jan said. "It's in a regular feature, edited by the paper itself."

"Do you think someone at the paper put it in?" Bob asked.

Jan shrugged and shook her head. "I went over there yesterday," she said. "But I couldn't seem to get anywhere. River acted as if I was a little crazy even to have brought it up."

Bob shook his head. "River's always wanting to keep things moving. That's just how River is."

"Well, he couldn't tell me anything about it," Jan said. "Or he wouldn't," she corrected herself. "And neither would Candace. But," Jan added, "she's actually coming over later to work on an article. I think I accidentally talked her into doing a story on our wedding when I was turning in our picture for the engagement announcement."

Bob smiled. "I didn't realize you were going to turn this into a celebrity affair," he said. He stuck his hand out as if he was warding off a group of phantom paparazzi. "Please, no pictures!"

"You're pretty good at that."

"I've had a few celebrity clients in my day," Bob said.

"Who?" Jan asked, her curiosity piqued.

"I could tell you that," Bob said. "But I'd have to have you sign a confidentiality agreement. And if you broke it, I could take you for everything you're worth."

"I thought you were already going to do that," Jan said, with a mischievous grin. "For better or for worse."

Bob squeezed her. "I am. And it was just the head of the Maine Blueberry Association. That's the biggest celebrity I've ever worked with."

"Oh," Jan said, giving him a fond swat. "Listen to you."

"So..." Bob leaned against the counter and looked back over the papers. "What's your theory? Who do you think is putting these messages in the paper? And why?"

"I'm just trying to think of *how*, right now," Jan said. "However crazy River thought I was, I can't imagine him sneaking a code into his own paper. And he's the one who signed off on everything, this issue. And it sounds as though he's been serving as de facto editor for the past few months. So Candace couldn't be doing it without his knowledge."

"And the idea of him letting Candace sneak codes in sounds even less likely than him doing it himself," Bob said.

Jan nodded. "That's right. So how in the world do they get there? Unless...," she said.

"I see an idea forming." Bob watched her with approval.

"They're not the last ones to touch the paper," Jan said.

"No?"

Jan shook her head. "The printing is done offsite. So that means somebody at the printer has control of the text of paper for at least some of the time. Perhaps many somebodies, depending on how many they have working on the *Penzance Courier* account."

"Can you find out who the printer is?" Bob asked.

Jan rattled through the nearest copy of the paper until she found a tiny line of text, barely visible, at the bottom of the front page: *printed by James Thompson and Sons.*

"Ah, Thompson's," Bob said, with a happy lift to his voice. "They've done some work for me over at the office."

"Really?" Jan asked.

Bob smiled at her surprise. "You might think it's a lawyer's job to help people navigate the legal system," he said. "But you'd be wrong. Actually it's our job to keep printers in business. We don't really work in law. We work in paper. Lots and lots of it."

"You do enough printing that you have to use the same printer as the newspaper?" Jan asked, still incredulous.

"We're probably not as large a client," Bob said. "But I'm afraid to say, even amidst that volume of paper usage, we still hold our own."

He opened a box of scones, pulled one out, and took a bite. "These scones are incredible," he said. "They make me want to marry you."

"Finally," Jan joked. "I thought you'd never ask."

Bob took another bite and closed his eyes, apparently lost in some kind of ecstasy.

Then he opened them again, all business. "Arnold Thompson's a great guy," he said. "Why don't you give him a call? Let him know you're a friend of mine. I'm sure he'll do anything he can for you."

"Even this close to Christmas?" Jan asked. The tearoom was open today and tomorrow, which was Christmas Eve, because they'd apparently become a holiday tradition with many families in town who loved to stop by for a bit of rest and quiet in the midst of their last-minute shopping. But would a printing company be open?

"If I know Arnold," Bob said, "he'll be working till the very last minute, trying to make sure everything's in order before the break."

He pulled his phone out, scrolled through it until he found a number, then scrawled it on the corner of one of the newspapers spread out over the counters.

"That's his direct line," Bob said. "He oversees all the projects that go through the place. If he's not the one who's in charge of the *Courier* account, I'd be surprised. But if he's not, I'm sure he can tell you who is."

Jan looked at Bob, momentarily distracted by how handsome he was in his blue shirt, and how kind he was being to her.

"What?" Bob asked.

"You're just so nice to me," she said.

Bob drew her into his arms. "You're only saying that because it's true."

When he released her, he looked quickly at his phone again. "I was hoping I saw that wrong the first time," he said. "But I didn't. I've got a meeting in ten minutes."

Jan's face fell. "I was hoping to talk with you about some details on the wedding!"

"I'll be free tonight," Bob said. "But really, honey, you know I'm going to love whatever you choose."

"But this is about the *scones*," Jan said. "I know you have opinions about them."

"Scones." Bob snuck another one from the container on his way out the door. "My vote on scones is yes."

"I wanted you to taste some!" Jan called after him.

"My vote on tasting scones is also yes!" Bob called back over his shoulder.

Jan shook her head, smiling as she listened to hear the door click shut behind him.

Then she looked down at the number he'd scrawled on the corner of the paper, picked up her phone, and dialed.

"Thompson and Sons Printing," a man answered. His voice sounded competent and even kindly, but it was also clear that he was all business, ready to get on to the next item on his list.

Jan quailed a bit. Explaining her suspicions about a code in the paper to a complete stranger suddenly seemed a lot less inviting than it had been to explain her thoughts to Bob. Especially after the reception River had given her at the paper itself.

But she wasn't about to give up, or hang up.

"Hello," she said. "This is Jan Blake. I'm trying to reach Arnold Thompson."

"You've got him." Arnold's voice had turned both friendlier and slightly more impatient. "What can I do for you, Ms. Blake?"

"Bob Claybrook gave me your name," Jan said. "I'm—" She hesitated, not sure how to describe herself to this stranger. But then she decided to go with the truth. After all, she was proud of it. And they were getting married so soon that she wouldn't get to say it for very much longer. "I'm his fiancée," she said.

At the other end of the line, she heard a happy rumble of laughter. "Well, what d'you know!" Arnold said. "That sly dog. He hasn't mentioned a thing to me. Although I haven't seen him in quite some time. I guess maybe because he had some other things on his mind. Well, congratulations to you. And please pass on my congratulations to him."

"Thank you," Jan managed to fit in.

"What do you know," Arnold said again. "I haven't even seen that come through the engagement announcements at the *Courier* yet. Now, what can I do for you?"

"Actually, I'm calling about the *Courier*." He had given her a perfect opening to broach the subject, but she still felt a little sheepish bringing it up. "You see, I think I've found something like a . . . code that appears in the paper."

"A code?" Arnold asked, his voice still friendly, but now highly quizzical.

"Bob's looked at it with me," Jan said. "And it seems like something more than random characters to him as well."

She had resorted to using Bob's name and a bigger vocabulary to help convince Arnold that she wasn't a bonkers conspiracy theorist. But listening to herself, she worried that her extended explanation would only serve to convince Arnold that both she *and* Bob were crazy.

"Well," Arnold said, his voice still friendly, but full of something that sounded like genuine consternation, "that sounds like something you might want to talk with River about."

"I have talked with River," Jan said. "And he told me that it wasn't possible that the code had been introduced by anyone at the paper. According to him, the only possibility was someone outside. And the only people I could think of who might have control of it beyond the editorial staff at the paper was someone on the printing side."

"On our side, you mean," Arnold said.

She had worried that he might be put off by the suggestion that someone had tampered with the paper at his end, but mostly he just sounded relieved. Maybe he was grateful to have finally caught the thread of this bewildering conversation.

"That's right," Jan said. "I was just curious if you might know of anything that could shed some light here."

"River says he doesn't know anything about this?" Arnold asked.

"That's right," Jan said.

"Well, I'm sorry not to be able to help you more," Arnold said. "But I'm afraid it's virtually impossible for us to print anything other than what the *Courier* sends over to us as their final product."

"But you do provide layout services?" Jan asked. "River mentioned something about that."

"We do," Arnold said. "But part of those services is a proof stage. We don't send anything to press without it being thoroughly vetted and signed off on by the client. And we've got a number of double-blind fail-safes to ensure that we don't deviate from their final copy, at every step of the way. Unless...," he said, a faint note of worry beginning to creep into his voice.

Jan heard a storm of tapping at the other end of the line. Then his voice came back, full of relief.

"Nope, nope," he said. "It's fine."

"What's fine?" Jan asked.

"I was just double-checking the actual printed version of the paper with our final approved copy from the *Courier*, with all the appropriate signatures," Arnold said. "To make sure there wasn't any variation. There shouldn't be, if everyone follows our system. But you know how systems are. As long as people are part of them—"

"—anything can happen," Jan finished for him, laughing.

"So, no," Arnold said, getting back to a businesslike tone. "I can tell you conclusively there were no changes made to the approved version of the paper here on our end. But now that I think about it," he said, a note of surprise in his voice, "I do remember this page. The one with the mystery story on it. Is that what you're talking about?"

"Yes." Jan's heartbeat quickened. "That's the one."

"There were some changes on it," Arnold said. "Last-minute changes. That's why I remember it. I believe I was the last one in the office, so I wound up inputting them myself."

"Do you remember who made that request?" Jan asked. "Who authorized those changes?"

She could barely stand to wait through the silence on the other end of the line as Arnold thought. But then he sighed.

"I'm sorry," he said. "I can't. Last-minute changes aren't unusual. Sometimes the editor calls. Sometimes Candace does. Sometimes it's another member of the staff."

"But the editor has to sign off on everything, right?" Jan asked.

"In theory, yes," Arnold said. "But when they're crunching to get something to press, I don't typically hold things up trying to get a secondary confirmation."

"And you're sure you can't remember who put in that particular request?" Jan asked.

Another silence on the other end.

"I'm sorry," Arnold finally said. "I don't right now. But if it comes back to me, you'll be the first to know."

CHAPTER TWELVE

So it's all right if I bring Brody?" Sasha asked.

"Of course, honey," Elaine said to her daughter over the phone. "He's your fiancé!"

"Thanks, Mom," Sasha said. "You're the best. Can I bring anything?"

Elaine thought back to the embarrassment of riches in the tearoom kitchen in the form of scones, and thought wryly of telling Sasha that she might bring a dozen more. But she knew that Jan already had the Christmas dinner all planned and probably halfway prepared for.

"Just yourself. And Brody, of course."

"We'll be there," Sasha responded, a happy lilt in her voice. "Love you."

"Love you," Elaine said.

She pressed the button to end the call, but she didn't set the phone to the side.

Instead, she took a deep breath.

Then, standing at the back window of her room, looking out over Chickadee Lake, she dialed again.

As she did, she rehearsed once more what she planned to say. She was going to start with a question, actually, before she said her piece. She wanted to give Nathan every chance in the world to explain what was going on. But even more than that, she just wanted to believe there *was* some kind of explanation.

With each ring, her chest tightened just a little bit more, part with the familiar anticipation of hearing Nathan's voice, and part with something new and unpleasant, the worry and mistrust that she'd been trying to ward off ever since she saw Nathan with the strange woman at the Odyssey.

When the line clicked to answer, she opened her mouth and drew in a single short breath, ready with her greeting.

But then the tinny sound of Nathan's voice mail came on, his voice deeper and more serious than she almost ever heard him speak in real life.

"...not available right now. Please leave a message," she heard through a fog of disappointment, laced with even more worry.

Through their whole relationship, Nathan had always tried to make time to answer the phone when she called, even if all he did was take the time to let her know he couldn't talk now.

That's what he'd done the last time they talked, uncomfortable as it was.

But now he wasn't even answering.

As she wrestled with these questions, she realized the voice mail prompt had just beeped. She almost hung up, but then hesitated. She didn't want Nathan to see that she had called, but not left a message. But she didn't have any idea what she wanted to say. At least not to his voice mail.

"Hi," she finally said, a few seconds after the recording had probably already begun. "This is Elaine." With effort, she tried to make her voice sound breezy. "Just giving you a call. Give me a try when you can. Okay."

Had her voice sounded too sad and uncertain at the end? Would he think she was upset and be alarmed? Or even worse, think she was upset and avoid calling her back?

Before she could spiral down even further into these thoughts, Elaine dropped the phone into her pocket and shook her head.

Then she padded downstairs, where she peeked into the east parlor to find that Rose had the morning business at the tearoom well in hand, moving comfortably and confidently from table to table, doling out tea and fresh helpings of clotted cream or jam.

But before Elaine could slip unnoticed into the kitchen, she saw one of the guests waving at her from a seat in the nook by the window.

It didn't take her long to recognize Vanessa van Dyke, this time wearing a loose burgundy sweater studded with tiny sequins that sparkled like the snow beyond the window, with a bright-red coat thrown over the back of her chair. But somehow, even with all that bright color in her outfit, it was the shine of Vanessa's hair and the sparkle in her eyes that really held the eye.

"Oh, hello!" Vanessa was saying. "Good morning! Elaine, right?"

Elaine smiled as she threaded her way through the other guests to greet Vanessa. "It's good to see you back here."

Vanessa grinned. "I wouldn't miss it," she said, then leaned forward confidentially. "Don't tell Macy, but this is my favorite place in town."

Elaine beamed at the compliment.

"I mean, this would be a charming spot for any town of this size," Vanessa said. "But to discover you take tea as seriously as they do in some of the finer tearooms in Europe . . ." She leaned back in her chair and shook her head approvingly. "It's like finding an undiscovered wonder of the world."

"I'm not sure I'd go that far," Elaine began.

"Well, luckily, you don't have to. Because I would!" Vanessa said enthusiastically.

"Well, thank you. How has everything been for you this morning?"

"Wonderful, wonderful," Vanessa said.

"I see you've economized to just one pot of tea," Elaine said, smiling.

"And it was wonderful. The country wildflower blend. A little taste of summer, even in the dead of winter."

"I do love that one," Elaine said.

Vanessa nodded with a mischievous grin at her empty plate, which was full of crumbs. "But what you can't see is that I polished off three scones today. Because I gobbled up all the evidence."

"It's important to eat a healthy breakfast," Elaine joked, trying to seem as sober as possible. "It gives you the energy you need for your whole day. Would you like another?"

Vanessa burst into laughter. "Oh my goodness. You know the way to my heart, that's for certain." Then she began to wave her hands in a gesture of rejection. "But no, no, thank you. Not today at least. I think I've done all the damage I can do this morning."

"Is there anything else at all we can bring you?" Elaine asked more seriously.

"Rose has taken very good care of me," Vanessa said. "You've got a real gem there."

"We know it. And we're grateful."

"I think I'd actually like to take the check."

"We'll be right out with that," Elaine said.

"And you know what else I would like?" Vanessa asked.

Elaine turned back.

"Would you happen to have a copy of the paper?"

Elaine scooped up the set of papers that she and Jan tried to keep the tearoom stocked with: recent copies of the *Boston Globe,* the *New York Times*, and the *Wall Street Journal.* Between them, just about any guest could find what they were looking for.

At first, Vanessa's face brightened. "Of course you'd have copies of all the papers!" she said with delight.

She shuffled through them, murmuring approvingly with each new addition. But when she reached the one at the bottom of the pile, her face fell. "Don't you have a copy of the *Penzance Courier?*" she asked.

Elaine's eyebrows shot up. How in the world had Vanessa learned the name of the local paper already? Especially if she'd never been to town before?

"Oh," Elaine said. "Well, of course. Let me see if I can find you a copy. Was there anything in particular you were looking for?"

"Just the latest edition," Vanessa said. "I always think it's great fun to keep up with the local news wherever my travels happen to take me. Don't you?"

Elaine reflected wryly that in most of her own travels, she'd simply kept up with the local news by moving in and trying to make a new life in a new place. "I'm sure we've got it. Just give me a minute."

"And I'd love to have the most recent one," Vanessa said again. "Macy didn't have today's yet."

"Let me see," Elaine said, heading for the back with questions crowding her head. If Vanessa was really only interested in the local color, what in the world did she think had changed so much around Lancaster that she absolutely had to have the most recent paper? The reality was that just about everything that happened in the area was advertised for months, or weeks, before it happened, so that nobody would ever have a chance to forget about the big sidewalk sale, or the Christmas-in-April food drive, or the eternal Tuesday night spaghetti suppers down at the Congregational Church.

But the guests were always right.

"Can you drop off the check for the table by the nook?" Elaine asked as she passed Rose on the way to the kitchen.

"You mean for Vanessa van Dyke?" Rose asked, half-squealing in excitement even though she was whispering. "Don't worry, I've given her perfectly normal service. But I can't believe she's actually here. Can you?"

Elaine smiled at the fact that Rose seemed to be a mystery fan too.

"Have you read her latest book?" Rose asked. "I'm not through it yet and I'm dying to ask her what happens. And also afraid that she'll tell me before I'm done!"

"I don't think you have to worry about her spilling the beans," Elaine said with a wink, and proceeded back into the kitchen.

Jan had vanished, but she'd left the evidence of her investigations that morning all over the counters: what looked like a year's worth of *Penzance Couriers*, spread out just about every which way.

Today's paper, Elaine suspected, was hidden there among them somewhere.

Quickly, Elaine sorted through them, trying not to disturb too much of Jan's pattern, if there was in fact a pattern to what just looked to her like a mess. But she had enough respect for Jan's quick mind to know that she didn't necessarily see everything that Jan saw. That was part of what made them such a good team, not just at the tearoom, but in so many other things.

Near the top of the pile she found the most recent issue. A number of the others had been marked with pencil, in places where it looked like Jan was hunting for more lines of code, not just in *The Crooked Lake Mystery* chapters, but throughout the paper.

But the most recent edition, Elaine was relieved to see, Jan didn't seem to have gotten to. Or if she had, she hadn't made any marks. It was as clean as it had been when it was delivered, although a little bit rumpled.

Elaine folded it up and took it back into the tearoom, where she handed it over to Vanessa. "Our most recent *Penzance Courier*," she said. "Only the finest for our guests."

Vanessa grabbed at the paper with surprising eagerness. By the time she said thank you, her nose was already buried in its pages. She held the check on its pretty hand-painted tray up to Elaine, with her credit card prominently displayed on top, without even looking up at Elaine again.

"Of course." Elaine tried to stay polite as she relieved Vanessa of the check and card. "I'll be right back with this."

"Thanks," Vanessa said again, but she seemed very distracted. Although Elaine paused by the table, she couldn't really bring herself to hover over a customer while she was trying to read, so after a moment, she headed back to the card machine to run the charge.

As she did, she could see Vanessa stop at a page and begin to pore over it, her expression fascinated and intense. But she was too far away to see which article had captured Vanessa's attention.

She sighed and looked down at the card. As she did, her eyes widened in surprise. The name on the card wasn't Vanessa. It wasn't even van Dyke. It was something completely different: Annabelle Hart.

Elaine's first reaction was a jolt of worry. Was Vanessa van Dyke trying to buy her scones with a stolen credit card? But then she realized how absurd that notion was. Vanessa obviously had plenty of money and plenty of credit.

What she didn't have, as Elaine and Jan and Rose and Macy's fanlike reactions to her had made so abundantly clear, was privacy.

Of course she traveled under an assumed name. She wouldn't want to give her identity away and have to deal with a possible fan every time she handed her credit card over to buy a latte or a tank full of gas. And Annabelle Hart was obviously a nom de plume, Elaine thought. It sounded like a character in a novel, or a name a girl might make up when she was young if she didn't like the real name her actual parents had given her. But it also sounded strangely familiar.

The card reader beeped, and the pair of receipts slowly printed out of the slit in the machine, both customer and store copies.

Elaine laid them both in the check tray, then carried it back to Vanessa.

As she approached, Elaine angled to get a glimpse of whatever it was Vanessa was reading. But when Elaine arrived, Vanessa clutched the paper protectively to her chest, as if it was something highly private that she didn't want a stranger's eyes to even glance over—a love letter, or a financial document.

What in the world did Vanessa feel that way about in the *Penzance Courier*? Elaine wondered. The scores of the local high school basketball teams? The advertisements for the pre-Christmas sales?

Still clutching the paper to her, Vanessa quickly added a tip that came to almost half the total bill and signed her name.

"This was wonderful," she said. "Thank you." But her bright smile seemed to Elaine to be directed at something beyond her, as if she didn't quite have the energy to focus on Elaine at that instant, but was looking through her, looking for something else.

"Thank *you,*" Elaine said.

As she turned away, she looked back down at the check, to see how Vanessa had signed it. Sure enough, *Annabelle Hart* was scrawled on the signature line.

"Hmm." Elaine was somewhat amused to have discovered the secret name of her august guest.

But as she dropped off the signed copy with Rose and went back into the kitchen, something struck her.

Annabelle Hart wasn't the only name that sounded as though it had been made up to entertain an audience.

So did Vanessa van Dyke.

So which one was real? Vanessa van Dyke? Annabelle Hart?

Or something else entirely?

CHAPTER THIRTEEN

The search engine whirled and whirled as Elaine waited for it to bring her back returns on the name she had just typed into her laptop: Vanessa van Dyke.

But before the returns page came up, her phone rang.

Elaine reached for it with a start, her heart pounding with the thought that it might be Nathan. She felt a twinge when she saw that it was her son, Jared, but she was still glad to hear from him.

But when she picked up the call, she heard a small voice on the other line.

"Grammy," Micah, her nine-year-old grandson, said. "I have a question."

"I told him," Lucy, his twelve-year-old sister, called in the background. "I already told him."

Elaine checked the time. Jared and Corrine must be making good progress on their cross-country drive by now, but it was clear the kids were starting to lose their patience.

"What's your question, honey?" Elaine asked.

"I don't live in Maine," Micah said.

"That's true," Elaine said. "But we love it when you visit."

"But I'm going to be there for Christmas," Micah said, clearly following the thread of some argument.

"I certainly hope so," Elaine said. "We can't wait till you get here."

"But will Santa know?"

"Know what, honey?" Elaine asked.

"Know where to find me!" A plaintive tone had entered Micah's voice.

"Oh, that's a good question," Elaine said. "Let's think about that. Santa can fly all around the world, right?"

"Right," Micah said.

"And he can jump down any chimney."

"And even if you don't have a chimney," Micah said. "He can come through the window."

Elaine smiled at what was obviously a modern hack of Jared and Corrine's to the Christmas legend.

"Well," she said, "if he can do all that, don't you think he can find you in Maine?"

There was silence at the end of the line. Then Elaine heard Micah announcing to the rest of the car, "Santa can find me! He'll find us in Maine."

"Micah," she could hear Jared saying in the background as the phone shuffled, probably as Micah dropped it. "Did you hang the phone up? Is Grammy still on the line?"

There was another brief scuffle, and the call ended.

With a smile, Elaine looked back at her computer screen.

Maybe, she thought when she got a look at the search results, they had taken so long to come up because about half of the entire Internet seemed to be about Vanessa van Dyke: fan pages, author pages at Amazon and Barnes and Noble, book clubs sharing about her stories, her own author page, newspaper articles dating back decades, and her own Wikipedia entry.

But as Elaine sifted through them, looking for the normal details of a life—where Vanessa grew up, where she went to college, even where she made her home now—she was surprised that she couldn't find anything.

Of course, that was all identifying information that could be dangerous if it fell into the wrong hands. And many celebrities were closed-mouthed about exactly those topics.

But as Elaine thought it over, she realized she knew at least some of those facts about many of her favorite movie stars or public figures. It wasn't hard to find out where a politician was born, or where a movie star went to school. Often they proudly included this information in their official biographies.

But on Vanessa's author page, there was almost no personal information: just the fact that she'd wanted to be a writer since she was a girl, and a list of her publications, all with helpful links to the sales pages of big bookstores, so that all anyone who was interested needed to do to buy was click.

Elaine knit her brows and tried another search: *Vanessa van Dyke* with *Lancaster.*

Apparently Vanessa had written a quite popular mystery about a death at an English country house owned by the Lancaster family: Penny, Jerry, Benjamin, and Blythe.

But she didn't find even a hint of any connection with Lancaster, Maine. Which was almost odd, since Vanessa appeared to have read at pretty much every other bookstore in the continental United States—and a good number of the ones beyond, where she apparently had fans in dozens of foreign languages.

"What about..." Elaine said to herself, typing in her next search combination: *Annabelle Hart* with *Vanessa van Dyke.*

Vanessa, she discovered, had once consulted on a TV show with the name Hart in the title. The Internet also helpfully suggested that Elaine might be interested in seeing a round of search returns matching Vanessa van Dyke with *heart* because Vanessa had evidently served as a celebrity ambassador for the American Heart Association. She'd also written, in her early days, a short but apparently beloved series that had attempted to bridge the gap between mysteries and romances, with a set of linked books that all contained the word *heart* in the title.

"No, no," Elaine muttered, frowning at the page of search results.

Then she straightened up and tried a new search: *Annabelle Hart* and *Lancaster.*

"Ugh," she said as the search results came back—only one or two pages, and probably mostly total junk.

But as she scanned the first few entries, she discovered that they weren't just advertisements automatically generated by her search. One of them was a genealogy site, which appeared to have information on both an Annabelle Hart and Lancaster, although it wasn't clear from the teaser blurb whether they really had anything to do with each other.

For all Elaine could tell, it might simply be an Annabelle Hart in Boston, who was related to a distant cousin who happened to spend some time at some point in Lancaster.

But when she clicked on the entry, it turned out to be an Annabelle Hart in Lancaster.

Was that just because Annabelle Hart was a more common name than Vanessa van Dyke? Elaine wondered.

Quickly, she opened a second window and did another search, for Annabelle Harts in Maine. There were only two more anywhere in the whole state.

"Hmm," she mused as she clicked back to her original search window.

As she did, she realized why the name Hart had sounded familiar to her when she first read it on the credit card.

The Harts were an old Lancaster family. Chester Hart, in fact, was around Jan and Elaine's age and had overlapped with them in high school for at least a year or two. And Elaine remembered running into other Harts in town as well. She thought she remembered hearing that a Hart was one of the original fishermen who had helped found the little village on the lake that had now grown into today's Lancaster.

And she also remembered that some Harts didn't talk much with some of the other Harts. Jan had pointed this out to her when one of the younger Harts was briefly lighting up the pages of the *Penzance Courier* as a local football star.

"Chester must be so proud," Elaine had said. "We'll have to congratulate him when we see him."

"I wouldn't do that," Jan told her. "Something went wrong in that family years back. You can never be sure which Harts talk to which other ones. I told Minnie Hart down at the salon that she was the spitting image of Irma Hart, who works in the high school cafeteria, and Minnie didn't speak to me for a month. Not even when she was cutting my hair."

"And Irma Hart's a pretty woman," Elaine observed.

"I know!" Jan had said. "I was trying to give her a compliment!"

Even looking at the family tree on the genealogy site, Elaine could see that there had been some kind of a split in the Hart family. Whoever had filled this section of the site out with the family information knew one branch of the family far better than the others, even though it looked as though there were plenty of Harts in the previous generations, and plenty of them still living.

One branch that came down from a great-uncle and seemed to include Jan and Elaine's friend Chester, was full of dates: birth, death, weddings, middle names. All the identifying details that helped make a genealogy complete. The kinds of things that you take for granted knowing about the people who are closest to you, but can be very difficult to unearth once they're lost.

But the other side, in comparison, was only a vague sketch. In some cases, whoever built the chart had known the number of siblings in a family, but only had the names of a few of them, leaving the other spaces blank, perhaps in the hope that someone else might fill it in in the future.

And it was on that side that Annabelle Hart appeared.

Whoever built the chart hadn't known much about her. Of all the fields that could be filled out: birth, birthplace, death, burial location, marriage, occupation, current location, contact information, only two were filled out—birth and birthplace.

According to the chart, Annabelle Hart had been born in central Maine. And recently enough that, under normal circumstances, she should still be living and in her mid-fifties.

Elaine looked up thoughtfully. About the same age as Vanessa seemed to be.

But after that chart, the trail went cold. The genealogical site didn't contain one other scrap of information on Annabelle or her relatives. The few who had died in the generation before Annabelle had burial sites out west, in California and Washington state, about as far away from Lancaster as you could get.

And there were no other meaningful returns in the entire search of Annabelle Hart and Lancaster, just junk sites and other noise.

There might be other Annabelle Harts in the world, but this was the only one who seemed to have any connection with Lancaster. And after she was born nearby, Elaine thought, she seemed to have vanished off the face of the earth.

At that moment, Jan barreled through the door carrying a giant stack of thick books. Elaine tried to get a look at what they might be, but Jan had picked them all up with their pages facing out and their spines hidden.

"Oh," Jan said. "I forgot all about those papers."

"I tried not to get them out of order," Elaine said, turning back from her laptop.

Jan shook her head. "Don't worry about it. Just fold them up."

She swept a swath of newspapers aside with her elbow, then dropped the stack of books on the counter and grinned at Elaine.

"I've got an idea," she said.

CHAPTER FOURTEEN

I've been thinking about it," Jan told Elaine. "And I can't imagine that anyone could have written that Crooked Lake mystery story unless they knew us back in high school. So I decided, we just better go back to high school."

She pulled the first book from the stack and turned it over, revealing the cover of the Lancaster yearbook for their freshman year.

"Oh my goodness," Elaine said. "Look at those haircuts."

"I know," Jan said. "Why didn't somebody tell us?"

"I think I remember my mother trying. But I was too addled to listen to her. Maybe from the fumes of all that hairspray I was inhaling every day to achieve the feathered look."

"Chrissy James used to brag that she used up a whole can of it up every two days," Jan said.

"I think I might have used a whole can of it myself," Elaine said. "The night of the homecoming dance. I don't think my hair moved that entire night. And I danced the whole time!"

"You did love to dance, didn't you?"

"It was a great time for music," Elaine said, flipping through the first pages of the yearbook until she came to a stop at a picture of an air band full of boys pretending to play cardboard instruments as some long-forgotten song was piped through the loudspeakers for them to lip-sync along to.

"Remember these boys?" she asked. "Thinking aloud?"

"I thought that was so clever at the time," Jan said. "I remember laughing and laughing. We went into English class, thinking we'd come up with a world-class example of a pun, and I remember Mrs. Fisher just *looked* at us."

"Look at this, look at this," Elaine said, barely able to hold in her laughter. "Did I really dress up as Joan of Arc for the French fair?"

Jan peered down at the blurry photograph, which appeared to show a youthful Elaine dressed as the famous heroine, complete with feathered cap, a cardboard sword, and foil armor.

"The photographic record does seem to suggest that," Jan said. "Unless you were just trying out some interesting new fashion ideas."

"I had to do anything I could to get extra credit in that class, I guess," Elaine said. "I always learned the vocabulary for the test each week, but somehow by the next week, I never even had last year's vocabulary down."

"That would make it harder to learn the language."

"Hence the cardboard sword," Elaine told her.

"Oh, Mikki Albright," Jan said. "Remember her?"

"How could I forget?" Elaine asked. "That girl never missed a day of school in her life. Not from the time she was in *kindergarten*."

"I always wondered if attendance was really such an accomplishment. It seemed to me the point of school wasn't just showing up. You're also supposed to learn something."

"You can't learn anything if you don't show up," Elaine pointed out.

"Fair enough," Jan said.

"Listen," Elaine said. "Does the name Annabelle Hart ring any bells?"

Jan looked up from the page she had been perusing, which was full of pictures of the cheerleaders, all stacked up like a cord of living wood.

"Well, there's Chester Hart," she began.

Elaine nodded. Quickly, she explained what she had seen on Vanessa's credit card, and what she'd found—and not found—in her search for the name on the web.

"It can be hard to find women after they marry, if you're looking under their maiden names," Jan observed. "She could be going by anything now."

"I know," Elaine said. "I'm just wondering how long she stayed in Lancaster. There are all these death dates in California on her side of the family, but that doesn't really indicate exactly when they moved."

"Do you think she could have gone to high school with us?"

"Someone neither you nor I knew?" Elaine asked.

The cousins looked at each other. It was unlikely, Jan knew, that in a school that had a graduating class of right around a hundred people there would be many people neither she nor Elaine knew.

But a strange look crossed Elaine's face. "If you're right that that story was written by someone in our school," she said, "then there were definitely things going on back then that I had no idea about."

"Let's take a look," Jan said, flipping to the index in the back of the yearbook, which listed every time each student had appeared in its pages, and on which page. "It's worth a try."

Her heartbeat quickened as she ran her finger down the G's until she found Hart at the top of the H's. But Chester was the only Hart listed that year.

"Maybe she was a few years ahead of us," Jan suggested. "Or a few years behind."

Elaine, she saw, had already picked up the next yearbook in the stack and was flipping through the index herself. Just like Jan, her eyes widened hopefully when she found the right section. Then the light in them died out as she found nothing.

Each of them picked up one of the last two remaining yearbooks on the counter, but neither of them found any more in them than they had in the original two they'd looked at.

"All we know is that she was born here," Elaine said. "She could have moved while she was a baby."

"I hate to say it," Jan said. "But one explanation for her disappearing from the record like that could be that she passed away."

"But there's no death date listed on the genealogy site," Elaine protested.

"They're hardly exhaustive. And a child who was lost that long ago—they could hardly be expected to leave any trace on today's Internet."

"Which is exactly what I found," Elaine said thoughtfully. "Hardly any trace." She sighed and began to flip idly through the yearbook whose index she had just checked.

"Oh my goodness," she said. "Do you remember this float in the Chickadee Lake Parade? The one where Jason Applebee painted himself gold so he'd look like an Oscar statue?"

"You know," Jan said, turning the page of her own yearbook, for their junior year, "I remember thinking at the time that I'd never forget that. And yet, until now, somehow I had managed to."

Elaine laughed.

"It took us weeks to make that float," she said. "So much chicken wire. So many colored squares of tissue."

"Wait," Jan said. "What's this?"

"What's what?" Elaine looked up.

Jan turned the yearbook around so that Elaine could see the face of a girl on one of the pages of formal pictures that were supposed to include everyone in an individual class.

"Barbara Bushwyck," Jan said.

Elaine looked at the picture, puzzled. The girl who looked back had a fresh, pretty face. "She looks familiar. But I can't really place her. I don't remember her in any particular club, or class...or even at a pep rally or football game."

"She was pretty quiet," Jan said, looking down at the picture. "Kept to herself. She was in a home ec class with me. Neither of us could figure out how to make the apron they wanted us to make from their 'beginners' pattern." Jan elaborated with giant air quotes around *beginners*. "I've sewed prom dresses since then that were less complicated."

"Was she the one who transferred here at the beginning of our junior year?" Elaine asked.

Jan gave her head a decisive shake. "No. That was Patti Schuler. When she first got here, she couldn't talk about anything but how she was going to leave as soon as she turned eighteen. Today," she said with a grin, "she's still in town. I guess Lancaster grew on her."

"I guess so," Elaine said. She looked down at the picture of Barbara, still puzzled. "How did I never know Barbara?"

"She was a few years behind us," Jan said. "She would have been a freshman when we were juniors."

"As if a junior would ever pay attention to a lowly freshman!" Elaine joked, and turned another page in the yearbook she was slowly working through.

"Well, it's possible she was paying more attention to you than you knew," Jan said.

"What do you mean?"

"Don't you remember?" Jan asked.

Elaine shook her head.

"She dated Jim our junior year," Jan said. "Before you did."

Elaine's brows drew together. "I'm not even sure I'd call it dating. I don't think we went out more than a handful of times."

"Well, Barbara went out with him more than a handful of times," Jan said. "I can tell you that from all that time we spent in home ec class. She was head over heels for him. I mean, she was just a freshman, and he was a senior."

"And on the football team," Elaine said. "He must have seemed like a combination of Thor and Santa Claus to her."

"Yep," Jan said. "Although it wasn't just hero worship. They really seemed like a good couple to me. She wasn't much interested in football, as I remember. Or trying to be friends with the popular kids. But I know she cared about him."

"And she might care about writing a mystery story about something that happened almost forty years ago," Elaine finished for her.

Jan smiled, pleased that Elaine had caught her drift. It was always a pleasure to work with someone who was as curious and quick as Elaine was. Especially when they'd known each other for years and could sometimes finish one another's sentences.

But Elaine didn't seem to like the conclusion she'd drawn from this one. Her brow scrunched and her eyes looked both worried and a little sad.

"I don't remember her at all," she said.

"But what about the girls who were juniors and seniors when we were freshmen?" Jan asked.

Elaine sighed. "You're right," she said. "I still remember them. Clarissa White, with her fabulous green eye shadow."

"And Karen Bolton, whose dad let her drive his Mustang convertible to school every morning, even though she only lived down the block," Jan added.

"But I didn't know personal details about them," Elaine said. "I only knew about them from a distance. The kinds of things everyone else knew about them. The kinds of things they *wanted* people to know."

"But," Jan said, "none of them stole your boyfriend."

"Nobody *ever* stole my boyfriend!" Elaine looked miffed just at the suggestion.

Jan shook her head. "I didn't say anyone did. But I wonder if that's how Barbara might have felt, after you started dating Jim."

"And I never stole Jim!" Elaine almost yelped.

"No, no," Jan said in what she hoped was a soothing tone. "Of course you didn't. It's just that high school kids don't always think completely straight about everything. Especially when you're a young high school girl, thinking about your first true love..."

"Do you really think she felt like I *stole* him from her?" Elaine asked. Then she shifted uncomfortably on her feet. "And that she's still upset about it, all these years later?"

"I don't know," Jan said. "It would certainly line up with *The Crooked Lake Mystery* story."

"I recognized those details about myself," Elaine said. "And the details about Jim. But it never occurred to me that anything else about it could be true."

"Well, not true, exactly," Jan said, hoping to comfort her.

"But you know what I mean!" Elaine exclaimed. "I had no idea anyone ever thought I was part of their *love triangle*." Her nose wrinkled in distaste even as she said the phrase.

Jan suppressed a smile at her cousin's well-developed conscience. It was one of the things she liked best about Elaine. But it was also somewhat amusing to see her worry over the morality of a decades-old high school romance.

On the other hand, though, Jan thought, it was clearly still on the mind of at least one other person in town.

Jan reached for Elaine's laptop. "Do you mind?" she asked.

When Elaine shook her head, Jan dragged it over to her side of the counter and began to tap away in the query bar of a search engine.

"There's a Barbara Bushwyck still here in Lancaster," she said. "On one of these old lanes just off the lake. If I'm not mistaken, that's actually where she grew up."

"And her name is still Bushwyck?" Elaine asked.

Jan tapped a few more keys, then looked up. "That's a good point. It sure looks like it. So she—"

"—may never have married," Elaine finished for her.

As Jan watched, Elaine sighed. Jan hated to see the weight that seemed to descend on Elaine's shoulders.

"Does it say anything else at all about her?" Elaine asked.

Jan did a search for Barbara Bushwyck in Lancaster, then scanned the results. "There's not much here," she said. "She's listed on a high school reunion website, but it looks like someone else must have added her. There's no picture or information in her profile."

"What about a social media presence?" Elaine asked. "Or a professional network?"

Jan shook her head. "I can see her address here in town, and there's still a phone number listed for her in the public records. But it's just not telling me much else about who she is now." She looked up. "But since she's right here in town, we could always stop by and talk with her. Maybe we could even get her to help us do away with some of my practice scones. I'm not sure it was totally realistic to think that Rose was going to be able to peddle six dozen of them to our regular customers in a single day." Jan smiled, hoping to get a smile back from Elaine. But Elaine's expression was still distant and preoccupied.

She was looking down at Barbara's picture, fresh-faced and young and so innocent, in the pages of their old yearbook. Thoughtfully, she turned the page, looking over face after face, until she had glanced over most of the students who'd attended the school that year.

She looked up. "I was hoping something else would jog my memory," she said. "Some other explanation, maybe."

Jan came around the counter to slide her arm around her cousin's waist and give her a comforting squeeze. "The situation is just so similar to the story in the paper," Jan said. "I can't imagine it's referring to anything else."

"Probably not," Elaine agreed.

She flipped the next page, where the listing of the year's activities began, with a giant photograph of several dozen kids who had built a giant fort in the school parking lot out of the snow that had been cleared after the big blizzard that year.

"The fort," Elaine said, her voice brightening. "Do you remember that?"

"I remember how you made it to the top of the hill and pushed half the football team back down before someone finally toppled you," Jan said, with a twinkle in her eye.

"It wasn't fair," Elaine said. "Billy LaLonde got hold of the back of my coat!"

"And you slid all the way to the ground on your rear end," Jan laughed.

Together, the two cousins stared fondly down at the picture, each of them lost in her own memories.

Then Elaine sighed and looked at Jan.

"Do you think she's been angry at me for all those years?" Elaine asked.

"I don't think you did anything wrong," Jan said staunchly. "Whether she's been upset all that time or not. And," she added, reaching for her purse, "there's only one way to find out."

CHAPTER FIFTEEN

Oh, it's this house!" Jan said, delighted. "I've always wondered who lived here. It's such a little treasure box. And look how they've done it up for Christmas!"

Barbara Bushwyck's address was only a few blocks from the tearoom, down one of the nearby streets that both Jan and Elaine were in the habit of walking down to get their daily exercise, or just to get a break from the familiar sights and sounds of the tearoom and home. Both of them had seen the snug little home dozens, if not hundreds of times in their meanderings.

It was a small Cape Cod, but with beautiful details: buff-colored siding, with shutters painted the same slate blue as Chickadee Lake just before a storm, and a bright, inviting red door. Well-trimmed yew bushes flashed the shine of evergreen below a load of Christmas snow, and the whole yard was dominated by another giant pine, over twice the size of the house. The branches of the pine were also weighed down with snow, but from under it twinkled the shimmering glass of white lights, not turned on yet by daylight. Another string of lights ran along the roofline of the house, and electric candles stood in every one of the little home's front windows.

On the red door hung a juniper wreath with blue juniper berries and a red bow that matched the red of the door perfectly.

"Now, how did she ever get such a perfect match on these reds?" Jan asked.

When Elaine didn't answer, Jan glanced at her. But from Elaine's expression, she wasn't sure Elaine had even heard the question. She was staring intently at the door, as if she was willing herself to see through it—or to be anywhere else in the world but where they were.

"Well, she certainly has an eye for detail," Jan said.

"If she's the one who wrote that story," Elaine muttered, "she definitely does."

Jan put her hand on Elaine's shoulder to steady her while she rang the doorbell with the other.

They stood waiting on the porch for so long that Elaine finally took a step back. "I don't think anyone's home," she said, with relief.

But when Jan reached to ring again, Elaine grabbed her hand. "Don't ring twice!" she said. "It's rude."

"Not if nobody's home," Jan pointed out, pulling her hand free.

But before she could ring again, the door swung open.

At first Jan thought it must be Barbara's mother. The resemblance to the girl they'd known in high school was striking, but she looked to be years older than they were. Her hair had gone totally white, and her hands cramped with arthritis.

"Hello?" she said.

"Hello," Jan said warmly, as Elaine hesitated on the step behind her. "I'm Jan Blake. This is my cousin, Elaine. We were hoping to talk with Barbara Bushwyck. Is she available, by any chance?"

The woman's face broke into a bright smile, clearly delighted at the prospect of visitors. "I'm Barbara. Jan, of course. I haven't seen you in years, but you haven't aged a day! And Elaine," she said, looking over Jan's shoulder without any kind of flicker in her smile at all that Jan could tell. "I thought you two might be Christmas carolers. Although it is still early for that," she said, looking up at the sun, which still hung quite high in the sky. "But this is even better. Please," she said, stepping back from the door to let them pass. "Come in, come in."

She ushered them into the hallway, which was decorated with lovely swags of fresh juniper and what looked to be antique lace, in which a collection of white china child-angels were cleverly scattered, peeking out from what seemed to be their own tiny juniper Christmas forest.

"Your house is so lovely," Jan said. "These Christmas decorations are just wonderful."

"I've collected them from all over the world," Barbara said, looking over her shoulder as she led them into a small sitting room where a beautiful tree glittered in the corner, filled with blown-glass ornaments and strings of glass beads. "Those angels in the front hall are from Denmark."

"Beautiful," Jan said.

Barbara sank down into a comfortable chair with a medical support pillow at her back. "Please, have a seat."

Jan sat nearby on a pretty Victorian loveseat, while Elaine stood, holding out the container of scones they had brought with them.

Matter-of-factly, Jan took the scones from Elaine and yanked on Elaine's sleeve to get her to sit. To her relief, Elaine did.

"We brought some scones," Jan said. "From the tearoom."

"You know," Barbara said, "I've always wanted to get over there. But getting out for me these days..." She held up her arms, showing her prematurely crooked fingers. "Not always that easy."

"I'm so sorry to hear it," Jan said.

Barbara smiled. "Well, I certainly got my travels in while I had the chance," she said. "And now I'm glad I did."

Jan opened the box of scones and pulled out one of the beautiful floral-print paper tea napkins they always sent along with their to-go orders. "Can I tempt you with a scone?" she offered.

"Oh my goodness," Barbara said. "It looks like there's more than one kind here. What am I looking at?"

Jan pointed as she explained the contents of the box. "This is a strawberry with white chocolate and strawberry glaze. And this one is candied orange peel, with cinnamon streusel chunks."

"Orange and cinnamon. Very Christmassy," Barbara said approvingly.

"Do you think so?" Jan asked, her voice rising with a hint of worry. "I didn't want it to seem too Christmas-themed."

"But it's Christmastime," Barbara said.

"The truth is," Jan confided, "I baked these as practice for the ones I want to serve at my wedding. It's after Christmas.

Not long after. But I don't want the wedding celebration to get too mixed up with the holiday."

"Ah," Barbara said. "I see. May I?"

Jan smiled as Barbara reached for a strawberry and white chocolate scone, with her signature cross-stitch frosting.

"Oh, this is wonderful," Barbara said. "Just wonderful."

Jan beamed as Barbara took another bite, then set the scone down on her pretty napkin.

"But tell me, what brings you here?" Barbara asked. "I don't think I've sat down and talked with either of you girls since high school."

"Well, but that was only a few years ago, right?" Jan joked.

Barbara laughed. "Sometimes it feels that way."

Jan laid the box of scones aside on a nearby settee and glanced at Elaine, who had been uncharacteristically quiet this whole time.

Elaine was sitting stiffly on the edge of the couch, her eyes moving around the room with nervous energy, as if she wasn't sure quite where to look.

When Elaine didn't pick up on Barbara's prompt, Jan looked back at Barbara and smiled. "It's a long story," she said. "But have you been reading *The Crooked Lake Mystery* that's been coming out for the last few weeks, in the *Penzance Courier*?"

"You know what?" Barbara said. "I've been meaning to subscribe to the *Courier* for ages, but I've never gotten around to it." She leaned forward. "Now, what is the story about?"

Jan glanced at Elaine, surprised. Even if Barbara hadn't written the story, Jan had assumed there was a high chance she'd read it. Especially when they got to the house and realized she was a virtual shut-in. But if Barbara wasn't familiar with the story at all, Jan wasn't really sure where to begin.

Barbara glanced from Jan to Elaine, quizzically. Her glance seemed open and friendly, but was it really possible, Jan wondered, that Barbara hadn't read the story? Or was she just claiming ignorance, for her own reasons?

Beside Jan, Elaine stirred. "It seems...," she said, then trailed off as Barbara looked directly at her. "It seems to be about the time that we were all in high school together."

"Oh!" Barbara's eyes brightened. "That sounds interesting."

"Now," Jan said, having finally hit on a way to bring up the old love triangle that might not be too embarrassing for everyone concerned, "do I remember that you and Jim Biggers were an item back in high school?"

Barbara broke into a wide smile. "Jim. Is he part of the story?"

"You could say that," Elaine said.

"Have either of you girls been in touch with him?" Barbara asked. "I think the last I heard of him, he'd moved out to California to a navy base. And he and his wife had just had a little baby boy. Although by now, I imagine, he might be quite grown up."

"I can't say I have," Jan said, and glanced at Elaine, who shook her head.

Barbara sighed. "Well, yes, we did date," she said. "To tell you the truth, I was head over heels for him. Just head over heels. He was my first love, you know."

And your last? Jan wondered, looking at Barbara's hand, which was free of any sign of a ring.

"I thought I remembered you dating for most of the early part of our junior year," Jan said.

"My freshman year," Barbara said quickly.

For all her attempts to play the relationship off as long-ago, she certainly remembered the details, Jan thought.

"That's right," Barbara said. "We dated through Christmas, into the new year. And then we broke up just before spring, I think. Because I had been dreaming about going to the spring dance with him. But we never actually went to it."

Jan felt a jolt, and suddenly understood a tiny bit of how Elaine must have felt, hearing the details of her own life laid out in someone else's story. Jan clearly remembered Elaine and Jim attending that spring dance together. They had double-dated with Jan. But oddly, that detail hadn't been part of the story in *The Crooked Lake Mystery*, even though it would have been an excellent plot point, Jan reflected. Was it really possible that Barbara didn't remember Elaine had attended the dance with Jim? Especially if she had been as eager as she said she was to attend the dance with him?

Apparently, Elaine found this as hard to believe as Jan did. She shifted in her seat. "I actually went to that dance with Jim. Maybe you remember that?"

Barbara looked down at her hands. "I didn't know that," she said. "I didn't go to the spring dance at all."

Jan felt another zing of curiosity as more pieces began to fall together in her mind. Was Barbara telling the truth? And was that why the detail didn't appear in *The Crooked Lake Mystery*? Was this actually confirmation that she must be the author?

"But I can't blame you," Barbara said with a smile. "I think probably any girl in school would have been happy to go to that dance with him."

If she was nursing a secret grudge, Jan thought, she was giving the performance of a lifetime.

Beside Jan, Elaine took a deep breath. "Jim and I didn't date for long," she said. "I didn't even realize that you two had been together earlier in the year. I hope that didn't cause any hard feelings."

"You know," Barbara said, her brow knitting, "I did know that you and Jim had dated. It was hard to miss, even if I didn't go to that dance. And he asked you out just a week after he and I broke up. But I knew that wasn't your fault. Whatever else Jim might have been, I know he was true to me while we were together. He was just—like that."

"Yes, he was," Elaine said quietly.

"Do you mind me asking," Jan ventured, "why the two of you broke up?"

Barbara sighed. "You know, I think I may have just been too serious for him. I was only fifteen, but I thought I wanted to marry him. And that might not have been a bad thing to aspire to," she said with a smile. "I mean, in a few years. Jim was certainly the kind of man who would have made a good husband."

She shook her head. "But he was just a kid himself. I think he just wanted to have a good time. Not be so serious."

Jan glanced at Elaine. To her, that sounded exactly how Elaine had described her relationship with Jim—not so serious.

"But we had been very close," Barbara said. "And shared a lot of our thoughts and feelings. So I think it was hard for him, too, breaking up with me. That may be why he moved on so fast with you, Elaine."

"Hmm," Elaine said, thoughtfully.

"Is that why you came?" Barbara asked. "Because you were worried about hard feelings? From all those years ago?"

"This story in the paper," Jan said. "It seems to bear some resemblance to your story with Jim, and Elaine."

"Isn't that strange?" Barbara said, in a wondering tone.

"We just wanted to see if you knew anything about it," Jan said.

"I wish I did," Barbara said. "Now I'm curious to read it!"

On a small table beside her chair, a tiny alarm pinged. She looked over the arm of her chair, picked up a pillbox, and popped open one of its compartments. "Oh dear. I'm out."

Beside the pillbox were a small collection of prescription bottles. She picked one up and tried to open it, but couldn't get her cramped fingers to work. After a minute, she held the bottle out to Elaine.

"Would you mind?" she asked.

Elaine quickly opened the bottle and let a pill rattle into Barbara's hand, which Barbara quickly took.

"This arthritis," Barbara said. "If I'm holding a grudge against anything, that's it. I never expected to have this much trouble with it so early in life."

"I'm sorry to hear that," Jan said. "And it must be tough on your own."

"I'm lucky though. A girl who lives next door comes over and helps me with little things when I need them. Like sorting these medicines. Or the Christmas decorations. We get along."

"Wonderful," Jan said.

Barbara had a kind twinkle in her eye. "I never did marry. I trained to be a teacher, but while I was in school, they were recruiting teachers to teach the American children of foreign service workers all over the world. So I decided, why not give that a try? I had always thought maybe I would meet a man who would take me all over the world. But it turned out, I went on my own. That's where all these Christmas decorations came from."

"That's so interesting," Elaine said. "My husband and I lived all over the world as well."

"It sounds like we have more than one thing in common. You should come back one day and we can swap stories."

"That sounds good," Elaine said, with her first smile since they'd walked into the place.

"But only if you bring me back more of these scones," Barbara added with a wink.

"Well," Jan said, "you can absolutely keep these. There are three more in the box."

"Breakfast, lunch, and dinner," Barbara joked.

"I can't promise they're exactly health food," Jan warned.

"I think a little taste of joy every now and then is always healthy," Barbara said, popping the last bite of the strawberry scone into her mouth. "But please do come back to visit. With or without scones. I'd just be happy to see you, to tell the truth."

"Oh, we'll be back," Jan promised, rising from the loveseat as Elaine rose beside her. "And we won't wait another few decades, either."

With a bit of difficulty, Barbara rose herself and showed them to the door. "Come back anytime," she said as they stepped back out into the snow. "I'm always glad for the company."

"What do you think?" Jan asked Elaine when they were out of earshot and turning their steps toward home.

"I'm glad we went," Elaine said. "It felt good to get things out on the table with her. And I'd actually love to hear more about her travels. Who would have thought that two girls like us, from tiny old Lancaster, would wind up living all over the world?"

"Do you believe her?" Jan asked. "That there are no hard feelings?"

Elaine crunched through several steps on the snowy sidewalk before she answered. "I want to," she said. "I think I do."

"I believe her too," Jan said. "I don't think she even knew that story existed before we showed up on her doorstep."

"It certainly seemed that way to me. But I'm not sure I like what that means."

"What do you mean?" Jan asked.

"It turns out," Elaine said, "that we're right back to where we were before. Somebody wrote that story, though it doesn't seem to have been Barbara. If it wasn't her, who else in the world knew that story? And why would they have chosen to make me the villain in their mystery?"

CHAPTER SIXTEEN

Elaine sank into the chair in her room, feeling beat and exhausted.

When they'd come into the kitchen, Jan had given her cousin a close look. "I think you could use a break," she said. "Why don't you let me check in on how things are going in the tearoom, and you go upstairs and take a minute for yourself."

Elaine had opened her mouth to protest, but then decided that Jan was right. After everything that had happened over the last few days, all she really wanted was to have a seat, somewhere quiet.

So as Jan had bustled off, she'd climbed the stairs to her own room.

At first, it had been a relief to curl up in her chair and just spend some time looking around at all the things she had chosen so carefully to surround herself with in her own private space: pictures of Ben and her kids, her books, even the little area rug she'd bought recently to add a pop of color to the place, with a beautiful hummingbird drinking from a bright hibiscus woven into the pattern of the fibers.

But even here, she couldn't seem to escape thoughts of Nathan. And it wasn't a mystery why: from where she sat, the snapshot of the two of them he'd recently had framed and given to her was front and center in her view, perched under the lamp on the little table beside her bed.

She tried to keep from looking at it, but no matter what she did, her gaze always wandered back.

It was so frustrating, she thought. After two days of wondering and sleuthing, she was no closer to knowing anything about the author of the story in the *Penzance Courier* that contained so many of her personal details. And she still didn't have any clue about the personal detail that had been most on her mind all that time: what in the world Nathan had been doing with the woman at the Odyssey, and how he'd spent his time since then. For all her efforts, the only thing she seemed to have learned was that Jan was probably right that there was some kind of crazy code embedded in the printed version of the Crooked Lake story. And that wasn't a clue that helped solve anything, Elaine thought ruefully. Just another mystery.

Finally, she couldn't take it any longer.

If she couldn't stop looking over at that photograph, she could at least do something about it.

Glad to have finally thought of something she could *do,* she got up from her favorite chair, walked over to the photograph, and turned the frame facedown on her bedside table.

As she did, her phone began to ring inside her purse.

When she fished it out, it was still ringing. And there was another picture of Nathan: this time, the one that came up whenever he called.

After staring at it for a few rings, she hit the button to answer.

"Hello?" she said.

"Elaine," Nathan said. Her heart gave a little flutter as it still did every time she heard his voice, even after all the months they'd been dating. But he didn't sound like himself: rushed, perhaps nervous, even a little uncertain. "So glad I caught you. What are you up to?"

Elaine looked around her room. She didn't really have a good answer for that question. "Just home."

"Well," Nathan said, "I know it's short notice, but I felt bad about missing dinner the other night. I wanted to see if you might let me make it up to you by taking you to lunch today."

Elaine glanced at her clock. It was almost noon. "What time were you thinking?" she asked.

"How about now?"

Elaine took a deep breath. Jan, Rose, and Archie could handle the tearoom, she knew. But some part of her still hesitated. She had been ready to have it all out with him last night. And she'd felt hopeful about it.

But now she wasn't sure she wanted to deal with any more mysteries. Especially not one that had the potential to make her feel the way it felt to see Nathan with that other woman.

Still, it was hard for her to refuse him.

"Elaine?" Nathan persisted. "What do you think? Could you meet me at the diner in ten minutes?"

Elaine took a deep breath. "See you there," she said.

As soon as Elaine walked in the door of the diner, she wished that she hadn't agreed to meet Nathan there. It hadn't occurred to her at the time that the cozy, neighborhood atmosphere that she usually enjoyed there meant that it would be virtually impossible to have a private conversation. She could only ask him directly about the woman she'd seen him with if she wanted half the town to hear her ask—and to listen in on what he answered.

But Nathan was already there when she stepped in, rising from the seat he'd taken in the back to wave to her with a big grin.

As she approached, he reached out to give her a hug and a kiss, as he almost always did whenever he saw her. Elaine tried to squeeze him back, but something about it felt off to her. It was as if they were actors playing roles, without the feeling behind it. Was it because of her, or because of him?

"I'm so glad you could make it," Nathan said, settling into his seat. "I've missed you this week."

Tart words rose to Elaine's lips, but she held them back. "It sounds as though you've been busy. What have you been up to?"

"I have been busy," Nathan said. "Things have been a little . . . " He looked away from her, almost as if he didn't want to meet her eyes when he thought back over the last several days. "Well, let's just say they've been crazy."

"Crazy how?" Elaine asked.

"Oh, you know how things can get." Nathan's eyes darted off in another direction but still never locked with hers, as they almost always did when the two of them were together.

"Tell me about it," Elaine invited.

"Oh, I don't want to bore you with the details," Nathan said. He leaned forward and met her eyes finally, but they didn't seem open and curious, as they usually did. Instead, Elaine had the distinct, uneasy feeling that he was trying to change the subject.

"I'm always interested in whatever you're up to," Elaine said. She smiled, trying to keep the conversation light despite the weight growing in her gut. "Because I'm interested in you."

Nathan smiled. "Well, it's funny you should say that," he said. "Because I have to admit, I'm interested in you."

But he hadn't, Elaine noticed, answered her basic question. "So," she asked, "what *have* you been up to?"

Nathan sighed and shook his head. "I don't really want to talk about it right now," he said. "Do you mind terribly? It's just been a stressful couple of days, and I don't really want to relive them."

The hairs on the back of Elaine's neck stood up. He'd never refused to tell her what he'd been doing before. If anything, he seemed to save his adventures up just to tell her, however small they were: helping a kid figure out what size nails to buy during a trip to the hardware store, or captaining an auction with a hundred people all barking bids at him in the same room.

And this didn't seem to be an unreasonable request. In fact, it sounded a lot like Nathan: reasonable, open, and able to talk about his feelings, which was a rare quality in a man, and one that Elaine had grown to value.

She might have just been grateful that he was able to express himself, and let the conversation go on from there—if she hadn't just seen another woman kissing him the day before.

"All right," she said, and sank into an uncomfortable silence.

Nathan glanced across the table, apparently trying to read her face. By this point, Elaine was doing very little to hide her discomfort. But Nathan chose to press on as if it were just a normal lunch.

"So, how are things going over at the tearoom?" he asked. "The last time we talked, I think Jan was talking about..." He trailed off, looking to Elaine to help him. When she didn't, he started to guess. "Was it the table arrangements?" he asked.

Elaine nodded. "That was a few days ago," she said. "She had this idea that we could get vintage teacups for every guest as wedding favors."

"How many guests was she planning on having?" Nathan asked.

"That's the problem. I think she may wind up inviting the whole town. For that many teacups, we'd have to scour every vintage shop from here to Boston."

"Sounds like a big wedding," Nathan said, his brow furrowing. "How do you feel about that?"

"It's Jan's wedding," Elaine said. "So whatever she wants is fine with me. That's the first rule of weddings, in my mind. It's not up to anybody but the bride."

"I mean, big weddings in general. How do you feel about them?"

Elaine looked at him in consternation. They'd rarely talked about anything relating to marriage or weddings before. It was such a loaded question, especially with Bob and Jan's wedding coming up so quickly, that they'd both naturally seemed to sidestep it whenever it came up. What in the world was Nathan doing now?

"I think it depends," Elaine said, trying to make it clear from her expression that she'd prefer to change the subject—to just about anything else.

"Depends on what?" Nathan persisted, doggedly.

"I guess it depends on a lot of things," Elaine said. *Now who's the one avoiding the question?* she thought. Did she seem just as evasive to him now as he had seemed to her a minute ago?

She sighed, relenting slightly. "If you've got a big family," she said, "I can understand how it would be hard not to invite all of them. And once you invite all that family, it might feel hard not to invite your own friends. After all, a lot of people are closer to their friends than their family."

Nathan nodded, seemingly grateful that he'd finally gotten her on a topic that she was willing to talk about.

"But I always like a small wedding best," Elaine said. "It just feels so much nicer when it's not a mob scene. To me, at least."

"That's what I think too," Nathan said eagerly, almost as if he thought the two of them were the only two people in the world to prefer small weddings.

"So do you have anything interesting coming up this week?" Elaine asked, picking up the diner menu in hopes that the gesture would definitively change the subject, even though she hadn't really needed to read the menu in years. She'd been there so often she knew it like the back of her own hand.

"What about, uh, destination weddings?" Nathan asked. "I always thought that was a way to keep things small. Nobody will come unless they really care about you. Maybe it doesn't make sense for a young couple just starting out, to spend all that money when they could use it to start out in life. But I always thought it might make sense for a couple who were a bit older and knew exactly who they wanted to have with them."

Elaine looked up from the description of the diner's excellent French dip, her mouth open in shock.

"A destination wedding," she repeated.

Was that what all this had been about? Was Nathan acting so strange because he had a ring in his pocket and he was about to propose to her in the middle of Kate's Diner, in front of the entire town of Lancaster?

But if so, what in the world had he been doing the day before, kissing some other woman?

It was one of the things Elaine had always liked best about Nathan, that once he got an idea or a task in his head, he didn't let go of it until he followed it through to the end. But on this topic, she thought he was about to drive her crazy.

"Sure," he said. "Like to Cabo. Or something really crazy, like the Norwegian fjords. I've always wanted to see the fjords," he added. "And I never have."

Elaine almost asked him flat out if he was talking about his own wedding, and what exactly he thought she might have to do with that. But in this state, she wasn't sure whether she wanted his answer, no matter what it was.

"I've heard the fjords are beautiful," she finally said.

"That's what I've heard," Nathan said. "I think it'd be good to see them, don't you?"

Elaine gave a brief nod and looked back down at the menu.

Oddly, she felt a strong urge to give Nathan a call and tell him about the incredibly strange conversation she was having right now—with himself. She was so used to being able to talk with him about anything, no matter what it was. And so used to him telling her any little thing she asked about.

Who was this stranger sitting across the table from her now?

What had he done with the real Nathan?

And what could she do to get him back?

"Oh, look at this!" Nathan said. "They've got a special on Chickadee Lake trout."

"That's interesting," Elaine said, without much conviction.

"Did I ever tell you about that time there was a giant storm on the lake, and my grandfather got caught in it?"

Elaine shook her head. "I don't think so."

"Well," Nathan started in, "you know my grandfather was a legendary fisherman."

"At least to his grandson," Elaine said with a smile to let him know she was just teasing.

Nathan smiled gratefully in return.

"So one day," he said, "my grandmother told him there was a storm coming and he shouldn't go out. But he never would listen to her, so of course he sailed right out to the heart of the lake."

And suddenly, Nathan was his old self again, telling a yarn with all the same fire and warmth and humor that Elaine was used to: his grandfather had sailed to the middle of the lake and almost lost his boat to the storm, but discovered, after he had ridden it out, that his nets were almost breaking with an incredible haul of fish, so many that it drove the price of fish down in town to half of what it normally was for several days—and he still made enough to buy his wife a diamond necklace, in apology for ignoring her warning.

"Although he did make sure to tell her as he was giving it to her, that if he'd followed her advice, he would never have been buying her a diamond necklace," Nathan said.

He reached for her hand, and her fingers closed over his at the table.

"I'm glad to see you," he said. "It's been too long."

Elaine just gazed back across the table at him, trying to hold on to the good feeling between them despite the questions swirling in her mind.

"I guess that's been my fault," Nathan said. "Hasn't it?"

Elaine smiled. "Do I look foolish enough to answer that question?" she asked.

"I don't think you've ever looked foolish a day in your life," Nathan said.

Elaine's mind flashed back to watching the woman kiss him in the restaurant yesterday. Would she have looked foolish to someone who was watching them, someone who knew the situation, if they had seen her then?

He squeezed her hand. "Now, about last night," he said.

Elaine's skin prickled with the anticipation of what he was about to tell her.

"There was something you wanted to ask me about, wasn't there?" Nathan asked. "What was it?"

Elaine stared steadily across the table from him.

"Oh," she said, "I'll let you know if I remember it."

He could hardly have been described as forthcoming, even about the simple questions she'd asked him early in the conversation. Before she asked him again, she wanted to see what she could find out on her own.

CHAPTER SEVENTEEN

Oh my goodness," Candace said as she stepped into the tearoom from the porch. "Even the decorations just coming up to the door are gorgeous."

"Thank you so much," Jan said, taking Candace's jacket from her and hanging it up on the coat stand near the door, which was carrying more and more outerwear the deeper they got into the winter.

Jan and Elaine had decorated weeks ago, and in the busy days that followed, the decorations had faded into the back of Jan's consciousness so that she barely saw them anymore when she came in or out of the house.

But peeking out one of the front windows, she did feel a sense of satisfaction and accomplishment.

Her pact with Elaine had been that they wouldn't try to reinvent the wheel every holiday season. Instead, they'd invested in truly beautiful pieces that could be used and reinvented season after season. With, of course, fresh greens, which both of the cousins far preferred to the fake ones that crowded the department stores every holiday season.

And luckily, since they lived near acres and acres of pine woods, beautiful greens were both plentiful and cheap. They could have as many as they wanted, if they were willing to go to the trouble of tramping through the woods to cut them themselves. And after that, it was just a matter of how much time they wanted to spend swinging from rickety ladders, hanging swags from the lip of the roof over the porch, or the big peak of the roof itself, or the porch railing.

But this year, they'd decided to go all out, with greens and twinkle lights festooning pretty much every line of the house, almost as if it had been turned into a magical creature of the forest itself.

The smell of pine was so strong that guests could smell it even before they turned up the walk to the tearoom. And once they slipped inside, as Candace just had, it didn't end.

Their big departure had been candles. Victorian homes and Christmases were always filled with them, in both stories and printed images from the time.

"But Victorian revival style almost never includes candles," Jan had observed as she thumbed through the Christmas catalogs that had started coming that year all the way back at the end of September.

"There may be a reason for that," Elaine had observed wryly. "Do you want to spend all of Christmas next to a dry tree full of lit candles, holding a bucket of water?"

"Well," Jan had said, "what if we don't put them on the tree, exactly?"

So this year, instead of adding new ornaments to their already vast permanent collection, the cousins had invested in candles. They'd filled the chandeliers in both parlors with colored tapers and hidden candles behind the scrollwork of the beautiful glass lamps and lanterns they'd collected over the years.

And then, as the Christmas season had begun in earnest, according to them, just after Thanksgiving, they'd begun to light them, filling the house with a cheery and genuinely warm glow, with a flickering life to it that was different than even the softest incandescent light.

"And look at the light in here," Candace said, rubbing her hands together to bring the warmth back into them. "I don't think I've ever seen so many candles burning at once. I would on my birthday cake," she said with a wink. "But I've laid down the law I can only have three from now on: one for last year, one for next year, and one for this year."

"I like that strategy," Jan said. "Please, come in."

She'd thought that Candace must have seen the standard Christmas decorations at the tearoom at some point before. There was the large swath of thick velvet ribbon that wound up the staircase, which of course was festooned with juniper; the white ceramic crèche scene, whose shiny surfaces all glimmered in the candlelight; the delicate glass ornaments, mostly birds and fruit and forest creatures, which they scattered throughout the garlands that graced the mantels and lintels of the old home, but always high enough that curious children could look but not quite touch. But apparently Candace hadn't seen them, so Jan took her on a tour of the hall and both parlors.

In the east parlor, Clifton Young, Rose's dad, who was enjoying tea with his girlfriend, Rae, flagged them down.

"Jan," he said, "I have to say, you've outdone yourself. I've been coming here since you opened, but I don't think it's ever looked better. Or tasted better," he said, nodding at his plate of pastries.

Jan beamed. Clifton was a loyal patron because he loved stopping in to see his daughter, but Candace didn't know that, and Jan couldn't have asked for a more perfect advertisement for the tearoom on a day when a reporter was visiting.

"I've got all my Christmas shopping done," Rae, who was also a friend of Jan's, added. "But it didn't feel like Christmas until we got here."

After thanking her friends, Jan settled down with Candace in a cozy corner of the west parlor, which was slightly less populated than the east at this point in the day, pointing out her favorites. "I always liked this little glass squirrel," she said, referring to the mischievous scamp hiding in the swag over the door as they entered. "Holding on to his little glass acorn."

"I'm not sure I could choose a favorite," Candace said. "They're all so wonderful."

Jan smiled as Rose came over and set a pot of tea down between them.

"What's this?" Candace asked as Rose poured a stream of hot, fragrant amber liquid into her cup.

"It's one of my favorite Christmas blends," Jan said. "Cinnamon, orange, and rosehip."

Candace let the aroma waft up to her, then closed her eyes at the scent of it.

"That does smell like Christmas. *Just* like Christmas." She opened her eyes and took a sip. "Delicious."

"And . . . ," Jan said, unveiling a plate of scones that she'd set on the table in preparation for Candace's arrival. "Something that's not Christmas at all."

Candace looked hopefully down at the crisscross pattern of frosting on the strawberry scones.

"What's this?" she asked. "I've never seen frosting like it."

"It's my own invention," Jan said. "I'm not sure yet if it's original, or a little crazy."

"No, it looks beautiful." Instinctively, Candace reached for a scone, then hesitated, laughed, and looked up at Jan. "Do you mind if I . . . ?" she asked.

"Of course," Jan said. "That's what they're there for."

"That's what I was hoping," Candace said. Her eyes lit up as she took a bite. "I wouldn't have thought it was possible. But these taste even better than they look."

Jan beamed. Candace was always polite, but she wasn't always enthusiastic.

"I can't quite believe you took the time to come do this story," Jan said, "so close to Christmas."

"Well," Candace said, "as soon as the holiday's over, we still have another paper to fill. And to tell you the truth, I'm tired of covering Christmas stories. I'll be glad to talk about something else. But this is also the perfect place to spend some time this close to Christmas. It's like the two of you figured out how to bottle the essence of a Christmas celebration."

Jan looked around at all the glitter and light that surrounded them. Maybe it was a reflection of the light of God coming into the world in the form of a little baby in a faraway cattle stall. But part of her wondered if all this glitz, much as she loved it, really captured the essence of Christmas. To do that, she thought, maybe more people would need to spend time in the out-of-the-way corners of the world today, with the kind of people who didn't have a roof to call their own. In fact, she thought, she should think about finding a way to do that more often herself.

"So," Candace said between bites of the scone, "your wedding tea. Will this be part of that?"

"You're helping me decide that right now." Jan smiled.

"I vote yes!" Candace said with a grin. She pulled out her paper and pen and began to scrawl notes. "Tell me where you got this idea. Is it a traditional part of tea cultures? Do the queens of England have wedding teas?"

"Not that I know of," Jan said. "I don't believe it's typically part of traditional wedding festivities, like the engagement party or the rehearsal dinner. But I don't see why it shouldn't be."

She was pleased to see Candace take this quote down, word for word. If she could spread the idea through Lancaster and the surrounding communities that wedding teas were now in vogue, or even a new part of any respectable wedding, it could become a whole new stream of income for the tearoom.

"Well, a tea seems like a perfect addition to any wedding to me," Candace said. "So much of a traditional high English tea seems suited to a wedding celebration. The fine china and silver. The beauty of the ceremony."

"Exactly," Jan said. "And the earlier hour..."

"That's another thing I was thinking about," Candace said. "Why do people stay up to all hours the night before a wedding? Why not have the gathering *before* the rehearsal? In the afternoon?"

Candace was practically doing both sides of this interview, Jan thought. She had worried a little bit in advance whether she'd be able to get her ideas across, but apparently that wasn't going to be a problem. "You took the words right out of my mouth," Jan said with a smile.

As Candace finished her tea and scone, Jan walked her through her dreams for the wedding tea. Even though the wedding was going to be in the heart of winter, she still wanted it to be full of hints of spring, and the tea would be full of them. She planned to let guests choose among a small array of teas, but all of them light floral blends, and herbal, so that the caffeine in them wouldn't wind any children—or adults—up before the rehearsal dinner. And the floral theme would continue with candied violets and pansies on the tea cookies, as well as rose petals baked into one of her scone recipes.

"But not every wedding tea has to have a floral theme," Jan said, warming to her theme. "We could do blueberries, for instance, and tie in with our Maine products. Blueberry jam, blueberry scones, blueberry and cornflower tea."

"Yes, yes," Candace said, scribbling away, and peppering Jan with questions each time Jan paused, like how children would handle the fine china, which prompted Jan to bring out one of the exquisite children's tea sets that she and Elaine hardly ever had a chance to use in the course of the tearoom's daily business.

"There was practically a whole industry in children's tea sets," Jan said. "And at an event like a wedding tea, you can have a children's table—chaperoned, of course—and give them a tea setting that was actually made just for them."

"Look how tiny these are," Candace said, handling the pint-sized cups and saucers.

"And children, as a rule, recognize how special they are," Jan said with a grin. "In our experience, children break less of our fine china than our adult guests."

"I think this is going to be a great article," Candace said, when the last drop of her tea had been drunk and she had helped herself to a second of the strawberry scones, to Jan's immense satisfaction. "It'll give people something to look forward to after Christmas. Remind them that there are still delights in the future, not just the past. And I love the idea of the wedding tea, myself. I have a friend who's getting married a few months after you are, and I'd love to tell her about it."

"*Please* do," Jan said. "In fact, if she'd want to come over and get a taste of what it might be like, I could make time to meet with her anytime in the next few weeks."

"I'll give her your information." Candace folded up her notebook.

"I did have one thing I wanted to ask you," Jan said. During their conversation, she hadn't just been concentrating on tea. The gears of her mind had been turning, still working on the problem of the code in the paper. And while she'd asked Candace before about the author of *The Crooked Lake Mystery,* she hadn't mentioned the code in the story to her—only to River.

But their conversation had been so friendly and open that it gave Jan the courage to broach the subject.

"What's that?" Candace asked.

Jan hesitated, then smiled. "I feel a little strange asking this," she said. "But do you know anything at all about a code that might be appearing in your paper?"

"A code?" Candace repeated, still friendly, but now curious. "What kind of code?"

Quickly, Jan told her about the messages she seemed to be discovering, hidden in the left-hand column of the paper.

"That's so interesting," Candace said. "Did you ask River about it when you talked to him?"

"I did," Jan said, then drew a breath, wondering what to say.

She didn't have to say anything, because Candace smiled when she saw Jan's expression. "I can imagine. And you're sure it's not just random?" she asked.

"I've actually spent a lot of time looking for similar patterns," Jan said. "In other publications. And in other parts of the paper. So far, I've found nothing."

"Other parts of the paper?"

Jan smiled. "You are a good reporter," she said. "That's right. The codes only appear in one section."

"Which one?" Candace asked.

"*The Crooked Lake Mystery*," Jan said. "As far as I can tell, there's been a code in several of its installments. But nowhere else."

Candace's brow furrowed in concentration. "And River told you he didn't know anything about this?" she asked.

Jan shrugged. "Pretty much."

"That's interesting," Candace said. "Because he's actually been quite hands-on with that particular story."

"Is that unusual for him?" Jan asked.

Candace nodded. "River's never been a micromanager, which actually helps make him a good editor."

"I always thought most people could do their jobs better if their bosses would just leave them alone," Jan observed.

"That's especially true for journalists," Candace said. "Sometimes you can't explain what you're doing until it pans out. And sometimes, after all the work you put in, it doesn't. If you've got to give an accounting for what you're accomplishing every day, you could never get anything done."

"But for this story," Jan said, trying to draw the thread of the conversation back to the question of the codes. "He was a bit more involved?"

"*Quite* involved." Candace didn't look too pleased about it. "To the point of making several last-minute changes, without the author's consent. Which the author wasn't pleased about, I can tell you."

Jan felt a little thrill go through her. She'd thought she was on the trail of the codes, but Candace had just inadvertently revealed that she did, in fact, know the identity of the Crooked Lake author.

"So you have been in contact with the author personally?" she pressed, trying to keep her tone as light and friendly as the rest of the conversation had been.

Her attempt failed miserably. At the mention of the Crooked Lake author, all of Candace's friendliness vanished, replaced by the surprise of the recognition of the revelation she had just made, followed quickly by suspicion. "I told you," she said. "I can't talk about that."

"I'm sorry," Jan said. "We just love that story so much. And also, it seems to contain some details that are very—personal—to our family. I didn't mean to pry."

By this time, however, Candace wasn't even trying to give her a polite reply. She stuffed her notebook into her bag and stood to leave.

Why could she possibly be having such a strong reaction? Jan wondered. It wasn't as if she...

Suddenly, a new thought burst into Jan's mind. What if Candace *was* the author? "Candace, I don't have any desire to violate anyone's privacy. If you're the author, I can promise you—"

"I already told you," Candace said, her voice now sharp with a real edge. "I can't talk about that."

Jan glanced around the parlor, grateful that it wasn't full of other customers to witness this performance, but feeling sick over the turn the pleasant meeting had taken.

"Candace," she began, but Candace had already slung her bag over her shoulder and was stalking through the twinkling lights of the tearoom, headed back into the bitter cold of the day outside.

CHAPTER EIGHTEEN

That sounds awful," Elaine sympathized.

"I'm so upset that she was unhappy," Jan said. "And she was supposed to be writing a story that would help us get more business. And it's almost Christmas Eve!"

Elaine, standing beside Jan in the kitchen, gave her a one-armed hug. But secretly, she was glad for the distraction from everything—including the fact that it was almost Christmas Eve.

Nathan was supposed to join them tomorrow night for the gathering they had planned for friends and family at the tearoom, after it closed that afternoon for the holiday. But from his actions over the past few days, she wasn't sure if he was going to show up with a wedding ring, which she wasn't at all ready to accept, or if he was going to show up at all.

So the question of the codes and the mysterious mystery author was a welcome change of scenery from the parade of worries that had been marching through her own head.

"Well," she said, "you might not have done what you meant to do in that meeting with Candace, but I think you accidentally found a big break on those codes."

"What's that?" Jan asked.

"It must be River," Elaine said. "Or he must have had something to do with it. Candace practically told you as much. What would he be doing to that story, last-minute, without the author's permission, if not inserting that code you found? How else would it have gotten there? Who else at the paper could have done it without him noticing? Whatever else we might think about Candace, you don't think she did it, do you?"

"No," Jan said slowly. "She was curious about the code. I don't think she'd ever heard about it before. She only got upset when I asked her about the story."

"I think River knows more than he told you the last time you went over there. And I, for one, would like to ask him about it." Elaine scooped up her keys from the counter, feeling grateful for an excuse to get out of the house. "How about it?" she asked her cousin. "Are you up for a country drive?"

When they walked into the office of the *Penzance Courier*, the place was virtually deserted, but Cookie still manned the front desk, and Elaine caught sight of River, bowed over some work on his own desk deep in the newsroom bullpen.

"You're down to a real skeleton crew," Elaine said to Cookie as they walked in the door. "Are they going to let you go home soon?"

"Oh," Cookie said, "you'd be surprised what comes up in these last few hours before the holiday." She gave a knowing grin. "And you'd be surprised at how many of them only the administrative assistant knows how to handle."

"Are you making your famous sticky buns this year?" Elaine asked. "I remember you bringing them to a cookie exchange a few years back. I would have traded all my other cookies for them."

Cookie laughed. "Not yet," she said. "They're only good when they're perfectly fresh. I get them all prepped, and I pop our family batch into the oven Christmas morning while the kids are opening their presents."

"Sounds perfect," Jan said. "Just let us know what time. We'll be right over."

Cookie laughed again. "Now what can I do for you two ladies today?"

"We were hoping to talk with River."

Cookie glanced over her shoulder. "You know," she said, "under normal circumstances, I'm always supposed to say he's busy. But I happen to know he just put today's issue to bed. And he's been in a good mood all day. I think Christmas must be getting to him. Why don't you girls just go on back?"

"Thanks," Elaine said, following Jan as she pushed through the low door that opened into the newsroom and threading her way through the empty desks to River's.

Just as Cookie had said, River looked up at the two of them with a beneficent smile.

"Jan, Elaine. Merry Christmas to you. What brings you here today?"

Jan sat down in the chair beside his desk, while Elaine stood beside her, then laid several of the papers she'd been sifting through for the past several days down on his desk.

"It's these codes," she said. "I've learned a few things about them since you and I talked last."

River's face changed at the mention of the codes, but not to annoyance, as it so often did. Instead, his features were pinched by anxiety.

"Oh?" He glanced down nervously at the papers she'd placed before him. "Like what?"

"Well," Jan said, "I've spent a lot of time with the newspaper since we talked, and I don't find anything else like them, anywhere else in the paper. Especially nothing the length of the message in this last installment, mentioning the meeting at the park."

When River glanced up at Jan, he looked to Elaine like a scared little boy. Was that what he was hiding?

"And," Jan said, "I understand that you made some last-minute changes to the last installment of the story. Changes the author hadn't even approved. And without the author's permission."

River looked from the paper to Jan, and back to the paper again, as if he was waiting for her to say something else.

When she didn't, his expression changed to the brash, assertive look she was more used to seeing from him.

"I don't see that you've really discovered anything here," he said. "It seems to me that we're back to exactly the same place we were when you last barged into my newsroom. Except that now your visit is keeping me from getting out of here for the holiday."

Elaine could see Jan shrink back under this contradiction, but to her credit, she didn't give up.

"Maybe you could tell me what the last-minute changes you made to this story were," Jan said. "If they didn't have anything to do with the code."

River sighed. "You know what?" he said, making a big show of rattling the most recent copy of the paper open. "All right."

Once he had the paper open, he swatted it down on his desk and jabbed his finger at the column of type that Jan had showed him earlier.

It was remarkable, Elaine observed, how quickly he found it. Almost as if he already knew exactly where it was.

"Let's just pretend," River said, "that your theory is true. There's some kind of code in this paper. Now tell me, what would you like me to do?"

"I'd like you to tell me anything you might know about it," Jan said.

"I already told you I don't," River said. "But let's say there's a code, and I'm the code reader. I look for it. I find it. What have I found? The name of a park in town. And something that may or may not be a time. If it's a time, is it 5 a.m.? Is it 5 p.m.? We don't know. *Because it's not a code.*"

River leaned back in his chair, looking satisfied for the first time since they arrived. "Or if it is, it's by a very bad code writer. If I'm trying to follow this code, I don't know what day they mean. And I don't know what time."

"Well, maybe," Jan said, "there's something more. Something we missed."

"But you said that these codes of yours only appear in *The Crooked Lake Mystery* installments. Am I right about that?"

"The only ones I've found," Jan admitted. "That doesn't mean there aren't—"

River sighed. "I'm sorry," he said. "I know you're good citizens of Lancaster, and I know you've cooperated with this paper before. But I just don't have the time to deal with this anymore."

"If you could just tell us—," Jan began.

"I'm sorry," River said firmly. "I just don't have the time."

Elaine could see Jan struggle as she sat in the seat at River's desk, torn between her natural politeness and the curiosity that had brought the two of them all the way out to Penzance on the night before Christmas Eve.

At this, Elaine touched Jan's shoulder, which seemed to break Jan out of her indecision. Jan stood up. "Thank you for your time," she said.

River, who was already deep into some other document in his computer, raised his hand in farewell as the two cousins turned back toward the door.

As they did, Elaine noticed a young woman at the counter, talking with Cookie. The woman wouldn't have held her attention for long, especially not with her outrage over the way River treated them still coursing through her veins, except for the fact that her posture was so strange. She seemed to be hunched over the counter and letting her long blonde hair fall over her face as if she were ashamed of something.

Or afraid someone might see her, Elaine thought. But why would anyone be afraid to be seen at the newspaper office? Especially on a day when so few people were even there to begin with.

But as Elaine looked steadily at the young woman, her suspicions were confirmed. Catching sight of Elaine and Jan, she started, then ducked her head even lower. Then she scooped up something that lay on the counter between her and Cookie and hurried out as Cookie called something after her.

"Did you see that?" Elaine asked.

"See what?"

"That woman," Elaine said.

Jan shook her head.

"She seemed very nervous. And she just took something from Cookie. I wonder if she had anything to do with—"

But as the two of them came around Cookie's desk, Elaine broke off to smile at the receptionist. "Thanks so much for making time for us," she said. "With the holidays and all."

"Anything for you, Elaine," Cookie said. "You know that."

"That woman who was just here. She looked upset. Was everything all right?"

Cookie's eyes lit up. Clearly, the interaction with the young woman had had an effect on her, and she was glad to have someone to talk with about it.

"I hope so," she said. "Did you see her? It was the strangest thing."

"Is she someone you know from the paper?" Elaine asked.

"If she's been here before, I've never seen her," Cookie said. "But she was scared as a lamb, poor thing. I've never seen one of our writers grab for a check the way she did."

"One of your writers?" Jan repeated.

"Is she a writer for the paper?" Elaine asked, almost in unison.

"Well, I guess so," Cookie said. "That's where I found her check, in with the author payments. One of the last ones to go out this year."

"You don't simply mail them?"

"We do with regular vendors and writers," Cookie said. "But there are some who prefer to pick up. Often, it means they can get the funds into their bank a little sooner, if it doesn't go through the mail first. It depends. We try to do whatever they ask."

"So this woman must have requested a pickup then," Elaine mused.

"I guess so," Cookie said. "But she didn't request it from me. I would have remembered that name, I can tell you that."

"What's her name?" Elaine asked.

Cookie grinned. "Well, I can tell you what her name *isn't*," she said.

She held a finger up and whirled around in her chair to root through a paper folder of checks and check stubs.

Then she whirled back and laid a check stub on the counter, including the piece where the recipient had signed, acknowledging acceptance of the funds, and the 12/23 date.

There, on the recipient line, in neat but slightly flowery handwriting, was written "Joy T.T. World."

"It's the author!" Jan said.

Cookie looked up at her, surprised. "Well, of course, honey," she began, but Jan had already made a dash for the door, with Elaine right behind her.

The *Penzance Courier* was on one of the main streets in town, which still didn't mean much in the way of traffic, because Penzance was basically the size of Lancaster. It didn't even have half a dozen traffic lights within the town limits.

Outside the office, a light snow fell through the afternoon light, and the streets were crowded with people, bustling in and out of the town's cute little shops, picking up their last treats and gifts for the holiday.

"You go that way," Elaine said, giving Jan a quick nudge to the left. "I've got this side."

"What did she look like?" Jan asked.

"Long blonde hair!" Elaine called over her shoulder. "Young woman!"

Walking as fast as she could without running down her fellow pedestrians, Elaine hurried through the sparkling snow, dodging walkers, strollers, kids giggling about the trinkets they'd picked out for their friends and family, and a small choir from the local nursing home, singing their hearts out on the old-fashioned carols.

About halfway down the block, just outside a candy shop out of which the strong scent of hot chocolate wafted, she caught a flash of straight blonde hair falling down the back of a woman in a camel coat.

"Excuse me," she said, picking up her pace to pass a young couple who were walking along arm and arm, apparently unaware of any of the other dozens of people who strolled down the street along with them.

That put only a pair of other pedestrians between her and the woman.

"Excuse me," Elaine said, zipping around a woman in a bright-red hat and a man in a plaid jacket.

She caught up with the woman on the corner, where people streamed in and out of the old-fashioned drugstore that had reopened recently, with all its vintage counters and cubbies intact, but now filled with interesting craft and gift goods.

Just before the woman stepped into the street to cross, Elaine touched her arm. "Excuse me," she said. Her heart was in her throat as she did it, but if this was the person who had written so many of the details of Elaine's life into her story, Elaine couldn't wait any longer to meet her—even if it did mean accosting a stranger on a snowy street.

The woman turned back in confusion, her blonde hair falling like a sheet of liquid gold over her shoulders.

"Can I help you?" she asked, her voice guarded.

But as soon as Elaine saw her face, she knew that the woman couldn't help her. She was pretty, with blue eyes and fine features, but she was around Elaine's age. Because the woman in the newspaper office had been so careful to hide her face, Elaine hadn't gotten a good look at it. But she was certain that she had been young, at least several decades younger than Elaine.

"I'm so sorry," Elaine said. "I mistook you for someone else."

The woman forgave her with a smile and started to say something, but Elaine had already barreled off down the street again, moving even faster than before, in hopes of catching up with the woman from the newspaper office, who now had a significant head start on her—if she had even headed off in this direction at all.

But when she reached the end of the next block, where the downtown ended at the small parking lot the city had built to accommodate cars that couldn't find parking on the street, she still hadn't seen anyone who looked even remotely like the woman she had seen.

Hurriedly, Elaine crossed the street, bustling up the other side while keeping an eye on anything she might have missed across the way: a figure hiding in a doorway, or just inside a store.

Maybe, she thought, Jan had caught her. But Jan had barely seen her. Would she even recognize her if she saw her again?

Just across the street from the newspaper office, Elaine caught sight of a familiar figure: Jan, hurrying toward her down the same side of the street.

"I got to the end of the shops," Jan said, breathless. "And then I came back this way thinking maybe she'd already crossed over."

Elaine smiled briefly at the thought that the two of them had made the same calculation, at opposite ends of the town, to wind up on the same side of the street now.

But neither of them had come back with the young blonde woman.

"Any luck?" Jan asked, although by the tone of her voice, Elaine could tell she already knew the answer.

Elaine shook her head, still scanning the crowd through the falling snow.

The woman had vanished.

CHAPTER NINETEEN

Oh my goodness," Jan said when she and Elaine stepped through the door of their house, shaking the snow from their coats and hair. "Vanessa van Dyke. I'm delighted to see you back here."

"I can't stay away," Vanessa said with a charming smile. "Not once I tasted your scones."

"But haven't you been seated yet?" Jan asked. "Rose!"

Rose, who had her hands more than full dealing with an almost totally packed west parlor, while Archie manned the east, looked over her shoulder, seeming slightly harried.

"Oh, no," Vanessa said. "Please, believe me, she did her best to seat me already. Rose is really very sweet."

Jan smiled at the fact that Vanessa had already learned Rose's name. Not much seemed to escape her—which was perhaps why she was such a good mystery author.

"I just wanted to spend a little time looking around the place before I sat down," Vanessa confided. "It's so much easier to see things when you're not just stuck in one place. Do you know what I mean?"

Elaine turned back from hanging her own coat up with a copy of the day's paper from the cashier's counter. "I wish I had a new edition of the paper to give you, but I'm afraid the *Penzance Courier* only publishes once a day," she said with a wink.

Vanessa laughed as she tossed the end of her scarf—this time a deep emerald green—over one shoulder and took the paper.

"You've been reading the *Penzance Courier?*" Jan asked. "Did you see that wonderful mystery in it? Elaine and I have been enjoying it so much, but of course we're not experts like you. I'm dying to know what you think."

"There was a mystery?" Vanessa asked, her eyes narrowing in puzzlement, as if that fact had totally escaped her. To Jan, this looked like an act—especially since so little escaped Vanessa. How could she have even leafed through a recent issue of the *Penzance Courier* and not noticed the serialized story, which took up two of the major pages? Especially if she was a mystery writer herself.

Maybe it was the mild skepticism in Jan's expression that brought Vanessa to her senses. Or maybe it really did take her a moment to recover the memory.

"Oh yes," she said. "That little mystery story."

"We know the writer used a nom de plume," Jan said. "I don't suppose there's any chance you had anything to do with it, did you?"

Jan had meant this as an absolute joke. After all, what would someone with the profile of Vanessa van Dyke be doing publishing her work in the *Penzance Courier* for pennies, when she could sell it elsewhere for a thousand times as much?

But to Jan's surprise, Vanessa's face turned utterly serious in an instant. "Now why would you think I'd have anything to do with that?" she asked.

Until that moment, Jan hadn't. But, she observed, Vanessa hadn't denied that she was the writer of the story.

"That's a lovely little story," Vanessa said. "I have to say I enjoyed it quite a bit. But it's not my style at all. I'd never have called the sun a "glowing orb," for instance. I'm more of a 'call the sun a sun' girl, myself. You know what? I think I'm ready to sit down. Do you have any more of those lovely strawberry scones?"

"Today the special is cranberry and chocolate," Jan told her. "With that same cinnamon glaze."

"You could put that glaze on anything and I'd eat it," Vanessa said. "Toast. Cornbread."

"Maybe I'll try that next," Jan laughed.

But although Vanessa's smile was still friendly, she couldn't seem to get away from Jan and Elaine fast enough.

"That conversation was...odd," Elaine said as she and Jan stepped into the kitchen. "Earlier she couldn't wait to get her hands on the paper. She was so eager to see it that I would have thought she'd read everything in it from cover to cover. And maybe even have it memorized by now."

"I can't believe she thought I was serious!" Jan sighed and picked up one of the scones from the plate that was piled high on the counter. "Oh, this is good," she said.

Elaine laughed. "We had a great baker here this morning. I'm going to see if I can get her to come on full time."

"Whatever price she asks," Jan said, "I'd say she's worth it."

"That's true," Elaine said. "No one bakes the way she does."

Jan savored the next bite of scone for a minute. But then she laid the rest of it aside. "Maybe writers are like bakers. They have certain expressions that only they would use."

"Like Vanessa just mentioned," Elaine said. "That she'd never use an expression like the one in *The Crooked Lake Mystery*."

"If she was telling the truth." Jan raised an eyebrow. "But yes. Except the other way around. Instead of phrases she'd never use, a phrase she'd always use. I've read articles explaining that different writers have very different vocabularies."

"Shakespeare actually invented thousands of words and idioms," Elaine said. "Or at least Shakespeare is the first place we ever see them written down."

"Well," Jan said, "I don't think Joy T.T. World was probably operating at quite that level. Although that would have added a whole new layer to the mystery." She smiled. "But maybe if we could think of an expression that gets used in the story frequently, we could search by that."

The cousins looked at each other.

"The light through the trees!" they both burst out in unison, then started to laugh. In practically every chapter of *The Crooked Lake Mystery,* there had been a description of light through the trees. Light in the morning, light in the afternoon, twilight as the sunset, even streetlight falling through the leaves. For some reason, the author couldn't get enough of it and clearly thought everyone else ought to be as enthusiastic as they were.

"What if we researched that?" Jan asked. "On the Internet. See what else we come up with."

"On it," Elaine said, grabbing her laptop from the counter and pulling it to her before tapping away at the keyboard.

Jan watched as Elaine squinted in concentration, then scanned the first few results that appeared. But when she saw the disappointment in her cousin's eyes, she came around the counter to see what had turned up.

Light through the trees might have been a characteristic tic of the writer of *The Crooked Lake Mystery,* but it was far too broad for an Internet search. The returns included everything from a leaf removal place right there in Lancaster to what advertised itself as the most extensive warehouse of chandeliers and other home lighting solutions anywhere on the planet. Not to mention an all-girl band called Light Through the Trees.

But not one book or author came up anywhere in the first pages of the search returns—let alone a mystery.

"I wonder if there's some way to narrow it," Elaine said. "What if we include *author,* or *mystery*?"

"It's worth a try," Jan said.

But when they added *author* to the search, the page filled up with hits on a book about farming, and when they added *mystery* to it, the page listed dozens of places where mystery writers had used the phrase in one of their books—dozens of mystery writers.

Jan sighed. "Apparently the author of *The Crooked Lake Mystery* isn't the only one who ever thought to use *light through the trees* in a story."

"Apparently not," Elaine said.

"So we'd need something quite a bit more unusual. Do you remember anything else?"

"I'm not sure," Elaine said. She drew one of the nearby copies of the *Penzance Courier*, which were getting more and more crumpled the more she and Jan went over them, toward her. It crinkled as she opened it again to the page where the mystery installment began, and pored over it.

After a minute, she looked up. "What about *a spoonful of hope*?"

"*A spoonful of hope*?" Jan repeated. "That's in the story?"

Elaine nodded. "I think I remember it a couple of times. The English teacher is always doling it out when she gives advice."

"Is it that unusual?" Jan asked. "I feel like I hear people say it around here all the time."

"You know," Elaine said, "I've heard it too. But never anywhere very far from Lancaster. I think it may be kind of a local tic."

"Then if we could find a writer who's used that phrase—," Jan began.

"—maybe we could find our local writer," Elaine concluded and began to type.

Jan looked over Elaine's shoulder as the search results came up.

"No, no," Elaine murmured, scrolling through hits on souvenir spoon collections and new age self-help sites. But then, on the second page of returns, she stopped. "Look at this." She clicked on a blog post. "It's an actual writer. And she's used the phrase."

The two cousins both read the text that popped up when Elaine clicked on the link, a blog post from a mom about what it was like to try to get back into shape ten years after she had her youngest child.

"It's not a mystery," Jan said. "But it's quite good writing. Is she just a blogger? Can you see if she writes any fiction? Or seems to want to?"

Elaine clicked around the site, but there was nothing that mentioned a book or any other writing projects.

"It's not actually a very big blog," Elaine said. "It looks as though she only posts every few weeks. If that," she added, clicking again. "Last Christmas she didn't post for almost two months."

"Wait," Jan said. "Go back to that entry. The Christmas one."

"What?" Elaine asked, clicking back.

"I thought I saw…," Jan began. "Yes!" she said, so excited that she actually pointed with her finger at the screen. "Look at that. It mentions the *Penzance Courier*."

"You're right. It looks like she was looking up Christmas service times in her local paper."

"Her local paper?" Jan asked. "Is this blogger here in Lancaster?"

"Hang on," Elaine said, clicking on the About tab of the blog, which they hadn't investigated yet. A picture came up of a friendly-looking woman with short strawberry-blonde curls, standing on the banks of what looked for all the world like Chickadee Lake.

"That's the marina, the Tuttles' marina, in the background," Jan said excitedly.

Elaine frowned at the blogger's profile. "She's got her full name listed here." She gave a worried shake of her head. "Hasn't she ever heard of Internet security? There's so much personal information on this blog. When she's coming and going, the habits of her family."

"She may think nobody but her friends are reading," Jan said.

"Yes, but the problem is this," Elaine said, typing the woman's full name, Adeline Barnhill, into the search bar, along with *Lancaster.*

Immediately, a name and address came up.

"It's that easy to find her," Elaine said.

"She's right here in town," Jan said. "We wouldn't even need to take the car. I don't know how you'd find a writer who's any more local."

"Me neither." Elaine grabbed her purse.

Jan reached for her own as Elaine headed for the door. "Are we going over there now?" she asked. "Could it really be her?"

"I don't know," Elaine said. "But between the same phrase and the mention of the *Courier,* I figure it's worth taking a little walk."

In the hallway, they found Vanessa again, shrugging into her own coat.

"Going so soon?" Jan asked. "I hope everything was all right."

"Well, this is embarrassing," Vanessa said, with a grin that told them she wasn't really embarrassed at all. "Everything was so delicious that I finished in about one gulp. And the place has gotten so full now I didn't feel right just lingering at a table like I have been. But where are you ladies off to? I would have thought it would be all hands on deck with a crowd like this."

Jan looked around. Under normal circumstances, Vanessa was right. All the tables in both parlors were now packed with happy patrons. But she also knew the kitchen was well stocked and that Archie and Rose were more than capable of handling it all on their own.

"We're on the trail of a mystery," Jan told her. "We think we might have discovered the identity of the author of *The Crooked Lake Mystery*."

"Ooh!" Vanessa said. "I read a bit more of that just now. It's such a well-told story. But truly, nobody knows who the author is? I would have thought that would be a secret that would be liable to get out quickly in a town this size."

Beside her, Elaine was still intensely focused on getting over to meet Adeline Barnhill. She already had her coat on and was slipping on her gloves.

Jan grabbed her coat from the stand as well. "Well, this author's identity is still a genuine mystery," she said. "Unless we've just cracked it. That's what we're going over there to ask."

Vanessa's eyes widened. "So it's a real mystery!"

Elaine gave her an impatient glance. The details about her life that had appeared in the paper, Jan knew, felt so personal that this story didn't seem to have anything to do with the fun of a mystery story for Elaine. "I guess you could say that," she said shortly.

"Well," Vanessa said, "what if I came? Would the two of you mind?"

Jan looked at Elaine. Elaine shrugged.

"People sometimes assume I must be kind of a detective myself, since I write mysteries," Vanessa said. "But that's not actually the case. I actually write them because I love mysteries myself. At heart, I'm really a reader. But it's not very easy to surprise yourself when you're the one writing the story. I'd love to follow up a mystery where I don't know the answer for a change."

Jan watched her for a minute, remembering Vanessa's strange behavior when Jan had guessed that perhaps *she* was the author of *The Crooked Lake Mystery*. It still didn't make sense that a writer as successful as Vanessa would bury a major work of hers in the pages of a country newspaper. But what if she had? Could her eagerness to go with them have something to do with it? Was there any possibility she was tagging along so that she could keep one hand in the "writing" of this story as well?

But none of this seemed to have occurred to Elaine. She had already opened the door and was stepping outside.

Vanessa's eyes, as she looked to Jan for permission to go with them, were open and friendly. Perhaps she really meant everything she'd just said.

"Why not?" Jan asked.

With a grin and a flip of her beautiful hair, Vanessa followed Elaine out the door into the chilly afternoon.

Besides, Jan thought, trailing after her, if Vanessa was up to something more than she said, spending additional time with her was the best way to find out. And no matter what she learned, it would still be fun to get to know the local celebrity a little bit better.

CHAPTER TWENTY

"Wait," Jan said as they came up the sidewalk, toward the familiar sight of Barbara Bushwyck's snug little home, which by this time in the twilight was aglow with twinkle lights and welcoming candles. "We weren't supposed to go to Barbara's place. Did we follow the directions to the previous address?"

She looked down at the GPS on her phone, which she had used as a quick check to verify the map of Lancaster she already had etched in her head, from the time she was just a girl. She knew all the streets in town, but she didn't always know where the addresses fell on which, so she was often grateful to be able to consult the GPS as a backup.

"No," Elaine said, checking the piece of paper where she had scrawled the address after reading it from the blog post. "This is it. Look."

"Who's Barbara?" Vanessa asked, sounding thrilled, as if Barbara might turn out to be an agent of international espionage who had coincidentally retired to the small town of Lancaster after tiring of her career pretending to be a cat burglar and debutante while actually collecting the secrets of diplomats and politicians around the globe.

Jan couldn't quite believe it happened, but although it was Vanessa van Dyke who had asked the question, neither of them bothered to answer. They were too focused on the identity of another author: the elusive Joy T.T. World.

Jan looked from the paper in Elaine's hand to her own phone. The numbers were very close, and both even. But they were a few digits apart.

Jan looked up at the street, scanning for the house numbers.

"It's the house next door," she said.

Beside Barbara's place, to the left, was a beautiful Victorian, simpler than the tearoom, but still an excellent example of the building style, with a slate-blue roof, slate-gray shutters, and white siding that showed off especially well against the sparkling snow. Unlike many Victorian homes, it didn't have any gingerbread trim around the line of the roof, which by summer could make it seem almost too simple, verging on austere. But winter itself seemed to have taken the time to decorate the home for Christmas this year, with gleaming icicles dripping from the roofline instead of wooden trim, and a layer of shining snow on the roof.

Most of the windows in the home seemed to be lit up with warm light, indicating a family scattered throughout the house inside. And through one of the lower floor windows, they could just make out the colored lights of a large Christmas tree.

At the sight of it, Jan hesitated. "They're probably getting ready for Christmas," she said. "Do you really think this is a good time?"

But Elaine was already marching up to the front door, and with a wink, Vanessa raced after her. Jan sighed, alone for a moment on the sidewalk that ran by the house. Then she followed them to the front step.

By the time she got there, Elaine had already rung the doorbell. As Jan mounted the few short steps to the little porch, the door opened. A woman with strawberry-blonde hair, much like the picture on the blog, but slightly longer now, opened the door.

At the sight of the woman, Jan's memory flashed back to the *Courier* office, where she and Elaine had seen the mystery woman and then chased her through the streets, unsuccessfully. This woman didn't fit the description Elaine had given her. If they were looking at the actual Joy T.T. World, who had that other woman been?

"Hello?" the woman in the doorway said, with a quizzical look.

"Hello," Elaine said. "I'm Elaine. This is Jan."

"And I'm Vanessa van Dyke." Vanessa stuck out her hand.

Jan had been wondering how Elaine would get Adeline to talk with her, but at the expression on Adeline's face when she looked at Vanessa, all of Jan's questions were swept away.

"Oh my goodness, Vanessa van Dyke!" she said, both of her hands rising to either side of her face in surprise. "Vanessa van Dyke! What in the world are you doing here?"

Then she stepped aside from the door. "I'm sorry," she said, although they were the ones who had just turned up at her doorstep unannounced. "What am I thinking? Please, come in, come in!"

She ushered them into a large, comfortable living room where the Christmas tree they'd seen through the outer window glimmered in a corner, and various toys and boxes were scattered across the coffee table, beside which sat a large tub of wrapping paper.

"Forgive the mess," Adeline said. "I'm just trying to get some wrapping done. I'm telling myself it's not actually last minute this year, because I'm doing it the day *before* Christmas Eve, not that actual night."

She smiled and gestured for everyone to please sit, which they did, taking their spots on the cozy set of stuffed couches and chairs that populated the room.

"Vanessa van Dyke," Adeline breathed. "I hope I'm not embarrassing myself. It's just that, you've been one of my favorite authors for years. So many people can write a good sentence, and so many authors can tell a good story. But a lot of times, the people who write a good story don't write great sentences. And the ones who write great sentences don't always seem to have much to say. But your books—I can never put them down. And they're also such great writing."

Vanessa smiled back at Adeline as if Adeline were the first person ever to compliment her writing. "Thank you, dear," she said. "That means so much. I'm so grateful to hear it."

"I'm so glad to meet you!" Adeline's eyes were shining. It wasn't until this moment that the surprise of finding Vanessa van Dyke on her doorstep seemed to wear off, and she thought to wonder why. "Now," she said, looking a little bewildered, "what brings you here?"

"Well," Vanessa said, with her million-dollar grin, "I hear that you're a writer yourself."

"Me?" Adeline practically yelped. "A writer?"

Vanessa nodded.

"We just came across an article on your blog today," Elaine said, leaning forward in her chair. "We wanted to ask you about it."

"My blog?" Adeline echoed. Her voice seemed to get higher with surprise each time she opened her mouth. "I don't think I've even updated that since Thanksgiving. And the last time I checked, I'd only had a dozen visitors. And most of them seemed to be from my mom's nursing home."

"Have you ever tried your hand at fiction, dear?" Vanessa asked.

"Oh my goodness," Adeline said. "I mean, I've thought about it, but…"

"It seems like everyone has a book stashed away in a drawer somewhere," Vanessa said with an encouraging smile. "Or just stashed away in the back of their mind."

Jan glanced at her. True to her word, Vanessa sounded like a reader at heart. She was asking questions like a detective. But what she was after was a story.

"I wish I had the time to write a whole book," Adeline said. "But with three kids and a very needy Newfoundland, I've got my hands full for the foreseeable future." A shadow crossed her face as she said this, and Jan noticed that she hadn't mentioned her husband. Was he part of the picture?

"A blog is a lot more my speed," Adeline continued.

"What about in the past?" Vanessa pressed. "So many people turn their hands to writing in college. It's always more fun to write a book than a paper. Especially if the paper is due soon! That was *my* favorite way to procrastinate, anyway."

Adeline smiled, but shook her head. "That's probably why you turned out to be a professional writer and I didn't," she said. "I'm afraid I don't have a hidden magnum opus anywhere. And I'm not sure you'd really want to read it if I did."

"We were curious about your blog because it seems to have some similarities with a story that was serialized in the *Penzance Courier* this winter," Elaine said.

"Really?" Adeline asked. "That's interesting. What kind of similarities?"

"Have you read the story?" Elaine asked.

Another shadow crossed Adeline's face. "I think I've heard some friends talking about it," she said. "But I'm afraid I haven't had much time to read recently. I took a second job this fall, when I got the kids all back to school. And it's been a little crazy around here since then."

"I'm Elaine Cook," Elaine said. "My maiden name was Willard. Elaine Willard."

It seemed like a non sequitur. But from the way Elaine watched Adeline's face after she said it, Jan understood what she was trying to do: surprise some kind of reaction out of Adeline if she was the writer of *The Crooked Lake Mystery* and just making up excuses to keep from admitting to having authored the story.

Catching her cousin's drift, Jan watched closely too. But all she saw was confusion and a desire to understand why the conversation had just taken such a turn.

"Are you two sisters?" Adeline asked.

Jan smiled. She actually loved it when she and Elaine were mistaken for sisters, since she often felt in her heart that in the deepest way, they really were. But she shook her head. "Nope. Cousins."

"The story contained some details," Elaine went on. "About..." She hesitated, then looked to Jan for help.

"About our family," Jan said. "Some personal details about our family that were actually quite surprising to see printed in the paper."

"How awful!" Adeline seemed to be perfectly sincere. "And did they use your *name*? Is that even legal?"

"They didn't," Elaine said. "But the details are still recognizable."

"So you can see why we might have been interested in the identity of the writer of the story," Jan said, still trying to soothe the situation for both Elaine and Adeline.

"Of course," Adeline said. "If that happened to me, I'd be on the hunt for the author as well. I guess what I don't understand is why you'd come to me. I'm so flattered you found my blog. But I'm hardly the most important writer in town." She glanced at Vanessa. "Especially not with Vanessa van Dyke here. Are you *moving* to Lancaster?" she asked, in a tone of wonder.

Vanessa smiled. "Just visiting," she said. "For the holiday."

"Do you have family in town?" Adeline asked.

Jan thought she saw Vanessa's smile waver as she shook her head. "Just a getaway. Your town is so charming."

"Well," Adeline said, baffled. "But it's only *Lancaster.*" She took a deep breath, seeming to collect her thoughts again, and looked back at Jan and Elaine. "I mean," she said. "Vanessa aside, there are much more accomplished writers in town than I am. I don't even go to the writer's meetings on Thursday nights down at the library. Evie Pagels writes a whole column every week for the *Courier* on goings-on about town. And I know that Goodman Young has published short stories in one of those literary journals down in Boston. There must be at least a dozen people in town who have published more than I have, *somewhere.* Any one of them would be more likely to have written a story for the *Courier.* So what brings you here? Why me?"

Deflated, Elaine looked at Jan. But Jan wasn't ready yet to give up. Regardless of what Adeline said, her writing was similar enough to the style of the writer of *The Crooked Lake Mystery* that she was the one whose blog had hit when they had searched for that characteristic line.

"It was actually something about your style," Jan said. "In the blog. Something that struck us as similar to the style of the author of the story in the *Courier.*"

"My style?" Adeline asked, laughing. "I didn't even know I had one."

"Oh, everyone has a style, dear," Vanessa said sagely. "It's just a matter of whether you recognize it or not."

"A certain phrase," Elaine said. "*A spoonful of hope.* It's used in your blog and also in the story."

"*A spoonful of hope*?" Adeline repeated. "I don't remember ever writing that. But it's nice, isn't it?"

"It is," Vanessa agreed.

"Nice, and unusual," Jan said. "Your blog and the story were two of just a handful of places it appeared."

"Really? I feel like I've heard people say it before." Adeline's brows knit as she sifted through her memory.

"I think it may be a local phrase," Jan said.

"But I've never heard it anywhere else," Elaine said. Jan knew this was saying something, because of all Elaine's extensive travels.

It wasn't until Vanessa chimed in with, "No, I believe that's quite unusual. Although I like it," that Adeline's face smoothed.

"How interesting," she said. "But still, I don't know that it's an expression I would have used."

"But you did use it," Elaine insisted. "It's clearly there, on your blog."

"Could anyone else have taken control of your blog?" Vanessa asked, with a little thrill in her voice. "Do you think there's any chance you might have been hacked? By a stranger, or by a friend?"

Jan looked at Vanessa in bemusement. It was definitely interesting to move through the world with Vanessa and the seemingly endless fantasies she could spin from the simplest of details. But what would it be like to *be* Vanessa, she wondered. Did Vanessa really believe that international spies and hackers were lurking around every corner? Such an imagination definitely lent a sense of adventure to everyday life. But in the long term, Jan thought, it sounded exhausting.

"Um, no," Adeline said, with a grin that was almost as bemused as Jan felt. "At least, I can't think why in the world anyone would do that. I haven't had enough money in my bank account for anybody to bother to steal it for quite some time. And even if that's what they were after, it's not as if I leave my financial details on my blog."

"But perhaps someone wanted to change your story," Vanessa said.

"They might be interested in doing that if my name were Vanessa van Dyke," Adeline said. "I guess you must have plenty of fans who would love to change something about one of your books. It's always so easy to care about your characters and believe they're real. But around here—I can't think of any reason for someone to go through the trouble to bother with my writing."

"There's nobody else?" Vanessa questioned. "Nobody else who has access to your computer, or your blog?"

Adeline gave her head a definitive shake. "Absolutely not," she said. "Just my daughter."

"Your daughter?" Jan repeated, sitting up. Her mind flashed back to the woman who Elaine had seen at the *Penzance Courier*. Elaine had said she was young. Young enough to be Adeline's daughter?

"June," Adeline said simply. "She's a great writer herself. That's actually how I know Goodman Young has been publishing down in those journals in Boston. She's been working with him, in an independent study this year, for credit at the high school. He's never worked with a high school student before, but he was impressed enough with her work that he took her on as her mentor." She grinned with pride at her daughter's accomplishments.

"I may not be a professional writer," Adeline went on, "but one thing I do know is that it never hurts to have a second pair of eyes on a piece of writing. So if June's around, I always have her take a look at my posts before I set them to go live. And she's always got great suggestions."

"Did she look at your post about trying to get back into shape?" Elaine asked.

Adeline gave her a somewhat strange look. "I'm not sure. Why?"

"Because that's the one that uses the phrase *a spoonful of hope,*" Elaine said. "Is there any chance at all that she's the one who added it?"

"If she made that suggestion, I probably took it," Adeline said. "I just don't remember."

"Do you think she might?" Elaine asked.

"She'd have a better chance of remembering something like that than I would," Adeline said. "She's got such a head for words. She's the real writer in this family."

"Is she around this evening?" Elaine asked. "Do you think we could talk with her?"

CHAPTER TWENTY-ONE

As soon as June walked in the room, answering her mother's call, Elaine drew a sharp breath.

Beside her, she could feel Jan look at her in surprise, but as soon as Jan got a look at the girl, Elaine could tell that she understood Elaine's reaction. June had the exact same honey-blonde hair and slight build as the woman she had seen earlier that day, hurrying away from the *Penzance Courier.*

But as the cousin's eyes locked in recognition, their reactions were overshadowed by June's astonishment at discovering Vanessa van Dyke sitting in her own living room, beside her Christmas tree.

"Oh my goodness," she said. "Mom. Oh my! Vanessa van Dyke. What in the world? Is this some kind of early Christmas present?"

Adeline smiled as June sank down on the couch beside her, and stroked her back, almost as if she was a much younger child and simply needed to be calmed—which was much truer, Elaine reflected, than the girl, who obviously wanted to seem adult at this moment, would probably like to admit.

"It's as much a surprise to me as it is to you," Adeline said.

"I'm just visiting town for the holiday," Vanessa said, as if that was the most natural thing in the world.

By now June had somewhat managed to collect herself. "You are one of my very favorite writers," she said. "My mom had practically a whole library of your books, so I read all of them, but now I've read more than she has. I've read the series you did about Diana Preacher, who solves mysteries about kids in the juvenile justice system."

"I always liked those," Vanessa said. "Although they never got the traction in the market I hoped."

"Masterpieces don't always get traction in the market," June shot back. "When Herman Melville died, *Moby Dick* had sold less than a thousand copies. And he'd decided to give up on being a writer. Can you imagine that? What stories we might have if he hadn't given up, but kept on writing?"

As June spoke, Elaine had a strange feeling that she was listening to two professional writers talk about their trade—even though June was still so young.

Vanessa smiled. "I'm going to take it as a compliment that you think the Diana Preacher series bears any likeness to *Moby Dick,*" she said. "Although I can't say I'd be eager to read the sequel to it." She winked.

"I'm just saying," June said. "The market can't always tell when something is great. At least not right away. And I think those books are great."

"They're not easy to find these days," Vanessa said. "I'm impressed you even managed to get your hands on them."

"I swapped for them," June said. "There's some good sites for that online. I get books at the library sale and then swap them."

Adeline smiled proudly. "Somehow June can always tell what the best ones are. Even when she hasn't read them."

"Well," June said, "you only have to read a little bit to tell if the author can write or not."

"You mean *you* can tell," her mother said. "Not everybody can do that."

"Which explains the otherwise inexplicable careers of a number of authors," Vanessa said, with a mischievous smile.

"Some of those Diana Preacher books I had to swap three or four other titles for," June said. "Good ones too. But they were always worth it."

"That's so kind of you to say," Vanessa said.

June's nose wrinkled. "I'm not being nice. I wouldn't be nice if the books weren't good. I mean, I wouldn't be mean to you. But I wouldn't say nice things about a book that was bad. Yours are really good. I mean it."

"Thank you," Vanessa said. "I hear you're something of a writer yourself."

Elaine would have expected June to perk up with pride at this, but instead her shoulders hunched and her eyes darted around the room, almost as if she was afraid someone might overhear them. Then June's eyes settled on her mother, pleading with Adeline to help her with the answer.

"I told them what a great writer you are," Adeline said in an encouraging voice. "How you always help me with my blog."

At this, a weight seemed to lift from June's shoulders. "Your blog?" she asked, looking back around the room.

Her mother nodded. "They were interested in a line I wrote in it," she said.

"Which line?" June asked.

"A spoonful of hope," Vanessa volunteered.

June listened to it with the air of a practiced professional, trying to decide whether she recognized an element of a story—and whether she liked it.

"Yes," she said after a minute. "I remember that. It's a nice turn of phrase," she added, without a trace of pride, just the professional's sober judgment of a piece of material. "People use it around here, but I've never seen it in any other book."

"You've got a very good ear," Vanessa said.

"Thank you," June said simply. Then she looked around, a question in her eyes. She seemed to know just as well as they did that it wasn't a good enough line to bring even Elaine and Jan to their doorstep, let alone Vanessa van Dyke.

Her mother, without saying a word, seemed to pick up on this. "They were interested in it because it reminded them of something else," Adeline said.

"Oh?" June asked, curiosity in her eyes. "What?"

"*The Crooked Lake Mystery*," Elaine said. "The one that's been serialized for the past several weeks in the *Penzance Courier*."

Suddenly, June's expression was full of suspicion so deep it bordered on panic.

"Did you have anything to do with that, honey?" Adeline asked.

June's eyes darted around the room as if looking for an escape hatch.

"It's okay," Adeline said. "You're not in any trouble. We just want to know who wrote it. Was it Goodman?" she guessed. "Did he let you edit it for him?"

At this, a strange flash lit in June's eyes, quickly replaced by her earlier deep worry.

Vanessa shifted on the couch.

"Maybe it would help if you understood why we're interested in the story," Jan tried. "You see, it contains some details about our family. Things we wouldn't have thought many people in town would know. So we'd like to talk to whoever wrote it, to understand why they'd use the details of someone else's family that way."

"I don't think we introduced ourselves," Elaine said quietly. "This is Jan. My name's Elaine."

At this, June started to look sick.

"I'd love to know who wrote the story too," Vanessa said. "But my curiosity's professional. It's such a great story. I'd just like to congratulate the author."

June looked from Vanessa, to her mother, to Jan and Elaine, and back to her mother.

"Go ahead, honey," Adeline told her. "Do you know who wrote it?"

June looked down at her hands. "I did," she said.

"You wrote it?" her mother and Vanessa exclaimed, almost in unison.

June nodded, then looked up, very slowly, as if not quite sure that the house around her would still be standing when she did. But the fact that everyone and everything was still there, just as it had been, didn't seem to come as much of a comfort to her.

She sighed.

"Honey," her mother said, reaching for her hand, "why didn't you tell me?"

"I wanted it to be a surprise," June said. "We've been having such a hard time this year since dad died. I knew you were worried about Christmas presents, and I wanted to have a little extra. I wanted you to know you didn't have to take care of everyone for a change. Someone could take care of you."

Tears had sprung into Adeline's eyes as June talked. She gathered her daughter up in a bear hug. "Oh, honey," she said. "You shouldn't have to worry about that. I'm so sorry. And thank you."

June hugged her back, then looked over at Elaine and Jan warily.

Beside them, Vanessa shifted. "But you're an author," she said. "Didn't you want to put your name on the story?"

June met her eyes. "It was the first time for me to be published," she said. "It was scary. I didn't know people were going to like it as much as they did. I was afraid they might even hate it. And I didn't know what that would be like at school, or in town, if they did. It was Candace at the paper who agreed to publish it. She's friends with Goodman, and he showed it to her. But I made her promise that she wouldn't tell anyone who I was. Not even River White."

"Well," Jan said, "she kept her promise."

June stared back at her, as if aware that this couldn't be the last of it.

"That story," Elaine said. "Did it just come from your imagination, or was it based on anything in real life?"

June looked down at her hands again.

"Honey?" her mother prompted.

"It bears a very strong resemblance to some stories we know," Jan said.

"And some very big differences," Elaine added.

"Yes," June mumbled.

"Yes what, honey?" her mother pressed.

"Yes," June admitted. "It's based on something."

"Barbara Bushwyck," Elaine said. "Who lives next door."

Still looking down at her hands, June nodded.

"It's Barbara's story?" her mother asked. "Well, that sounds nice." She looked around at the little group, confusion building on her face at the expressions on Jan and Elaine's faces, which made it clear that they hadn't seen it as nice at all. "June?" she asked.

June looked up, this time at Jan and Elaine. "You're right," she said. "I wrote Barbara's story."

"She goes over there all the time to help her," Adeline added. "They've become quite good friends."

"I was asking her what it was like for her in high school," June asked. "How things were different then."

"A writer's curiosity," Vanessa said, nodding approvingly.

But June just sighed, looking miserable. "I couldn't understand why she never got married. She's such a wonderful woman, and I know she was pretty when she was young. I thought at first that maybe she had never been in love. But I found out she had."

"With Jim Biggers," Elaine said.

June glanced at her but couldn't seem to bear to hold Elaine's gaze. "Yes." She looked down again. "In high school. And I think he would have been good for her. They loved each other so much. And if he hadn't started dating some other girl as soon as they broke up, maybe they would have gotten back together. And maybe her whole life would have been different."

"So you didn't just write a story," Elaine said. "You rewrote history."

"I guess so," June said. She looked up again, this time with some of the passion in her eyes that she must have felt when she was working on the story. "I just wanted to give Barbara a happy ending for a change. I wanted to get the Laney character out of the way so that maybe Jim could come back to her."

"I'm not sure that's really true love," Vanessa commented, "if a man won't come back to you unless you lock the other woman up."

"We were all just kids," Jan said.

"Was Barbara angry about this?" Elaine asked. "When you talked with her?"

June shook her head. "No. She acted as if everything was fine. But how could it be fine?" she asked. "She lost the only man she ever loved. And she was alone all her life."

"Not all alone," her mother pointed out. "She had you to tell the story to."

"It's not the same thing," June said. She took a deep breath. "All I could think about is how I would feel if Brandon and I broke up. I don't think I'd ever be happy again. Especially if he wound up with some other girl right away. I don't know if I'd ever get married either. I might be alone forever, just like Barbara."

"I know Brandon means a lot to you, honey," her mother said. "But you've got a lot of life to live yet."

June nodded gratefully, but looked over at Elaine with worry in her eyes. "I didn't mean to cause trouble. I guess I didn't think that anyone would recognize themselves in the story."

"Well," Elaine said, feeling deep relief over the fact that she didn't have an enemy in town who had been holding a grudge against her all these years, "I guess that's a testament to your powers of observation. And description," she added.

June gave her a wan smile.

"And it's not a bad thing that people recognized themselves in your story," Vanessa said. "Or that your story caused a stir. That's a good sign. A sign you did something right in the writing."

"Thank you," June said tentatively, but her eyes flickered back to Jan and Elaine. "You're not mad at me?" she asked.

Elaine shook her head, marveling at the way the young girl existed side by side with the observant young woman who had written the riveting story she and Jan had enjoyed so much in the *Courier*. The teenage years were a strange time. But maybe, she thought, there was a bit of a child and a bit of an adult in everybody, no matter what age.

"No, honey," Elaine said. "But I will tell you something. I know it's hard to believe, but there's a whole world waiting for you after high school. Even if you don't get married. I got married and Barbara didn't, but she and I both traveled the world. My husband's job is what took me, but she was able to go anywhere she wanted."

"That's true," June said, taking this in.

"I don't know if one is better than the other," Elaine said. "But I can tell you that if you're lucky enough to get to be my age, one day the things that are happening to you now may seem as far away as my high school life does to me."

"I guess it was a long time ago for you, wasn't it?" June asked.

Elaine nodded. "Yes," she said. "I've lived several other whole lives since then. And it doesn't seem far away just because of the distance in time. It's because so many amazing things have happened to me since then."

"Good and bad," Jan put in.

Elaine nodded. "Both good and bad," she repeated. "But looking back, I wouldn't trade any of them. And I wouldn't trade my life back in high school with the life I have now, because my life's been so full and rich since then."

"In high school," Jan said, "it feels like the whole world is happening right there. But it's not true. Really, your future life is waiting on the other side of it."

June looked from one of them to the other. "Thank you," she said.

"Thank you," Vanessa said. "For writing a great story."

"And for clearing up the mystery," Jan said. "It was pretty eerie to read the details of our own lives and not know who it was who had written them down."

"I'm sorry about that," June said.

Jan smiled. "I've just got one question for you."

Elaine looked at her, not sure what Jan could still be curious about now that they knew how the story had wound up in the paper.

"Did you include any kind of code in your story?" Jan asked.

Vanessa looked at her sharply.

"A code?" June repeated, almost as if she'd never heard the word before.

"Any kind of hidden message?" Jan asked.

June's brow furrowed. "How would I do that?" she asked, then glanced at Vanessa, as though checking to see if this was some kind of trick of the trade that all professional writers knew about.

But Vanessa's eyes were locked on Jan.

"No," June said. "I didn't put any messages in the story."

"Well." Elaine stood. "I know your mom's trying to get some presents wrapped. And it sounds like maybe you have some shopping of your own to do yet this year." She smiled.

June smiled back. "I have a thing or two I want to go out and get."

Her mother hugged her. "Oh, honey," she said.

"But no peeking!" June insisted. "I still want *some things* to be a surprise."

Jan, Vanessa, and Elaine made their way to the door and gave hugs all around.

"That is one very talented young lady," Vanessa said, after they'd exchanged good-byes and made their way down the walk.

"What an extraordinary story," Jan remarked. "In every way. I feel like she should write a sequel, now that we know the rest of it."

"I wouldn't be surprised if she did," Vanessa said with a wink.

But Elaine's eye had been caught by a couple across the street. At first glance, she'd thought it was Nathan, then dismissed the idea because the figure was walking arm in arm with a woman. But when the two passed under a streetlight, she could clearly see Nathan's signature black-and-white checked scarf before the couple slipped again into darkness.

"Nathan!" Jan said, then looked at Elaine. "Was that Nathan?" she asked. "Who is he with?"

"Who's Nathan?" Vanessa asked.

Elaine's heart lurched in her chest, but there was no way she wanted to discuss this now, especially not in front of Vanessa.

So she just shrugged and shook her head as the couple vanished down the street.

CHAPTER TWENTY-TWO

Let's see," Jan said the next afternoon, surveying the kitchen, which looked as if it had just been ransacked by Santa and every one of his elves.

Scones were piled in several stacks on the counters: cranberry cinnamon, chocolate cherry, and rosemary butter, with whole pieces of rosemary which mimicked the needles of Christmas trees. Giant vats of both delicious seedless raspberry jam and clotted cream sat out on the counter, surrounded by dozens of filled and empty ramekins, because so many plates were going out the door that the staff didn't have time to open the fridge door to pull the ramekins out. A huge ham sat on the counter as well, which Jan had been shaving herself every few minutes, to provide more for the servers to take out to their Christmas Eve tea crowd, which had been crowding into the house since the doors first opened that morning.

"Is there anything else we need?"

"Another five servers?" Elaine suggested, putting down the plates she'd just cleared from a customer in the tearoom and wiping her hands on her apron. "A bigger house?"

Jan smiled at her. "It's three thirty," she said. "Just half an hour more." She took down a large mixing bowl from the cupboard and set it out beside some cream and flour. "We'll be done soon."

"Are you going to make more scones?" Elaine asked her.

"I had an idea," Jan said. "I just wanted to try it out."

Elaine looked at Jan with a vexed expression. "For our private dinner tonight?" she asked. "You don't think we could just use what we've got here? Even with that army out there, there will still be plenty left by the time we close."

She gestured to the counters which, as she had just pointed out, were piled high with delicious victuals—enough for everyone they'd invited to their party that evening and probably three times more.

Jan hesitated. She had had an inspiration for a new twist on a recipe during a lull in the busy pace of the kitchen, and she knew the rhythms of the business well enough to know that she had plenty of time to experiment, but she also knew that Elaine seemed to have been on edge all day. Since last night, really, when they had seen Nathan on the street as they were leaving Adeline and June Barnhill's place. And she knew Elaine wouldn't be thrilled if she told her the truth now.

But she also wasn't in the habit of lying to Elaine, and she had no intention of starting now.

"It's an idea I had for the wedding," she said.

Just as she'd suspected, Elaine looked completely exasperated. "Now?" Elaine asked. "On Christmas Eve? In the middle of one of the busiest days of the year?"

Before Jan could answer, a knock came at the kitchen door. And before either Jan or Elaine said anything in reply, Vanessa poked her head in.

"How are you ladies doing?" she asked with a big smile. Her red hair was complemented by a bright-red turtleneck sweater, which looked to be made from something cozy: cashmere or angora.

Without waiting for an answer, she stepped into the kitchen. "Oh my goodness," she said, looking at the ham that stood before her on the counter. "The brown sugar crust is exquisite. You don't mind if I just…" She scooped up a piece of the brown sugar crust that had fallen onto the counter and popped it in her mouth. "Heavenly."

"It's got cinnamon and pineapple juice in it," Jan said. "The secret ingredients."

"And your love," Vanessa said. "And your talent. I think those are really the ingredients no other chef could replicate."

Jan smiled.

"I just wanted to pop in before I took off tonight," Vanessa said. "I do love the tearoom and your Christmas spread here is incomparable. But I have to admit, you two have become my favorite part of the place."

"That's so nice of you to say," Jan said.

"You know," Elaine said. "We have another event this evening, just for our family and friends. If you'd like to join, we'd love to have you." She looked around the packed kitchen. "As you can see, there's plenty of food."

"And Jan's hard at work, making more, I see," Vanessa said with a smile. But then she sighed. "I'm sorry, though. I've got somewhere to be."

"Really?" Elaine asked, delight and curiosity in her voice. "What have you found to do in Lancaster on Christmas Eve?"

"Oh"—Vanessa waved her hand—"nothing important. I hope you two have the most wonderful night," she said. "Thank you so much for everything. Merry Christmas!"

And she sailed back out the door.

The kitchen door swung open again, and both cousins turned, but this time it was Archie.

"Scone emergency!" he said. "The Whitmores had eaten their whole basket before I could even come back with their second pot of tea. And I think the Johnsons are on their way to eating an entire ham themselves."

Together, Jan and Elaine swung into action, a blur of activity that didn't stop until just after four, when the final checks were dropped at the tables and the families who had come to enjoy a holiday treat began to filter out of the place.

As Archie and Rose went to work cleaning up in the kitchen, Elaine found Jan gathering up silver and china in the now-deserted east parlor.

"I'm sorry I was a little short with you about the wedding scones," she said. "I know you're a wizard in the kitchen."

"Thank you," Jan said. "You know I'd never even think of starting them if I thought they'd interrupt the flow of the tearoom this afternoon."

"I know," Elaine said. "It's just that—all this planning for the wedding. I've been worried about you. It's not like you. I was so happy when you and Bob got engaged, but it seems like the wedding has taken so much of your attention and energy. You've already got such a good man, and I think the two of you are going to be wonderful together. I don't know why you feel this need to do anything else. Especially not *so* much else. I just don't think it's necessary."

Jan set the tea tray she had been carrying back down on the table. "Of course it's not necessary," she said. "That's why I want to do it."

When Elaine looked at her with surprise, she went on to explain. "I never got to plan my wedding to Peter," Jan said. "My mother planned the whole thing, just lemonade and cake in the church basement." As she spoke, she still felt the little pang she always did when she thought about her first wedding—and another pang, which she always felt when she thought about Peter, ever since he had been gone.

"It was lovely," Elaine said. "Simple, but lovely."

"But it wasn't *mine.* I love arranging things and getting the details just right. I didn't want to impose on my own children's weddings. But I always wished that I'd been able to do that for my own."

"I can understand that," Elaine said.

"And it's not just that I want to plan *any* wedding," Jan continued. "I want to honor *this* one. I'm not just trying to do something over, do it right the second time. I wouldn't be marrying Bob if I didn't think that he and I could have just as good a life together as Peter and I had. Not the same, but just as good. To me, that's a huge gift. And I want to celebrate. And celebrate it in style. Even if some people might not think it's dignified."

She winked at Elaine.

Elaine smiled. "Oh, no. I never said you were undignified. I'm all for being undignified, especially when we're celebrating. You watch. I'll be the first one out on the dance floor, doing the Electric Slide."

"I'll have to remember to have the DJ take that off the song list," Jan joked.

Elaine hugged her cousin. "I'm sorry. I didn't understand."

"Well, you do now," Jan said simply.

Elaine picked up the tea tray Jan had set down and moved toward the kitchen. "Well, I'm glad we've got that settled," she said.

Jan followed her, carrying a trio of half-empty teapots.

"But you know what we don't have settled?" she asked, setting down the dirty dishes and picking up the *Courier* from where it had been stashed in the corner to make room for the chaos of the day's big tea. "The code in the paper."

Side by side, the two cousins looked down at the column where the code appeared.

"I really don't think June had anything to do with it," Jan said. "Do you?"

"No. I think she told us everything she knew. She wouldn't have had control over the layout of the paper, anyway. And it's pretty clear that she stayed out of the business of the paper as much as she possibly could. I think that night we saw her over there may have been the only time she even set foot in the building, to collect her check in time for Christmas."

"I bet you're right about that," Jan said.

Elaine sighed, looking down at the paper.

As Rose and Archie bustled around them, Jan's finger trailed down the left side of the column one more time.

"Meet," she read. *"Sea Pine Park. Five OC."*

"C-E-P-T-T . . . ," Elaine read, following Jan's finger down the page. "*Hmm.* C-E-P-T."

She stopped and looked at Jan, her eyes wide with a thought.

"Cept?" Jan asked. "That would only be a word if it began with an S. Or if it had an *E X* before it."

"C E," Elaine mused.

"I don't think that's a word either," Jan said.

"But neither is *O C.* It's an abbreviation. For *o'clock.*"

"Yes . . . ," Jan said, still not catching her drift.

"What if," Elaine said, looking back down at the paper. "What if *C E* is an abbreviation too?"

"For what?" Jan asked.

"What's today?"

Jan looked at her as if she'd gone slightly crazy. "Christmas Eve," she said. Then she looked down at the paper herself in shock. "Christmas Eve!" she repeated. "Five o'clock, Christmas Eve!"

"Do you think?" Elaine asked. "It couldn't really be . . . "

"What time is it?" Jan asked.

"Four forty-five," Archie sang out from the kitchen sink, where he had rolled up his impeccable shirtsleeves and was elbow-deep in suds.

"There's only one way to find out," Jan said, and headed for the door, Elaine close behind.

CHAPTER TWENTY-THREE

Sea Pine Park was only a few blocks from the tearoom, so the cousins made it there in plenty of time.

The streets of Lancaster on Christmas Eve might just as well have been pulled off a Christmas card, or put on one. On the other side of the street, Jan and Elaine passed a group of well-bundled up carolers drifting from house to house, occasionally bursting out in a rendition of "Hark! The Herald Angels Sing" or "Good King Wenceslas" when they found someone at home. The blocks that led to Sea Pine Park were ablaze with lights, both over the streets and in the homes: outlining the roofs and porches of the beautiful old Victorian homes and twined in the bushes and trees. The sidewalks, which were usually wide and passable, were full of foot traffic, with curious children and pink-cheeked parents, and loud expressions of delight when families who recognized each other crossed paths on the street.

But just as they arrived at the park, Jan pulled Elaine back into the hedge of the house that stood alongside the park, squinting into the growing twilight of the short winter days.

"What?" Elaine asked, pulling her arm free.

"We don't want them to see us!" Jan said. "What if we scare them away?"

"Want who to see us?" Elaine asked, peering around the hedge, which was so tall it ended just above her head. "Do you see someone?"

"No!" Jan hissed. "If we can see them, they can see us!"

"Well, how are we going to see them without taking that chance?" Elaine asked.

"Hmpf!" Jan poked her own head around the hedge. "Okay," she said.

"Okay what?" Elaine asked.

"You see that play structure over there?" Jan asked. "The big wooden one?"

"The one shaped like a boat?"

Jan nodded with the crisp discipline of a military officer. "It's not too far," she said. "I think we can get to it without being spotted. And from there we should be able to see everything through the portholes."

"Okay," Elaine said.

"Go!" Jan gave her a little shove.

Together, the two of them burst from behind the hedge, dashed over to the large wooden boat, and ducked inside. From one of the portholes carved into the wooden sides of the play structure, they could see nothing but the flash of Chickadee Lake, stretching out to the tree line on the other side.

But from the pair on the side, they could see everything that was happening in the entire small park.

"Do you see anything?" Elaine asked. "I don't see anything."

As far as she could tell, the park was deserted.

"What time is it?" Jan asked.

Elaine looked down at her watch. "Four fifty-eight."

"Maybe they're just not here yet," Jan said.

"No," Elaine said. "Wait. Do you see that? Over in the trees?"

"Where?" Jan asked.

Elaine pointed to a stand of trees at the rim of the park, where the land dropped away into the lake. "There. Is there someone in the trees?"

"I don't see anything," Jan said. "What do they look like?"

"I can't tell." Elaine squinted through the darkness. "It's dark, but I thought I saw a flash of red."

Beside her, Jan squinted through her own porthole. "Oh, I see that," she said. "But are you sure it's a person? There are so many Christmas decorations around town these days, one of them might have blown loose and wound up caught in the trees, and—"

But she stopped short as the bit of red pulled loose from the pines. Even in the twilight, the shock of red hair and the pale face were unmistakable above the red sweater.

The cousins turned to each other. "Vanessa," they said in unison.

"Well, that would explain why she chose to spend her Christmas in Lancaster," Elaine muttered.

"How?" Jan asked. "What does it explain? Why is she here? How did she know to answer the code?"

"I don't know," Elaine said. "But she's standing right there. We could just go ask her."

Jan's hand clamped like a vise on her arm. "Wait," she said. "We still don't know who she's meeting. We don't want to scare them away."

As she said this, a car pulled up to the park, idled by the curb for a moment, then shut its lights and engine off.

"Someone drove to the park?" Jan asked. "Almost everyone in town can just walk."

"Maybe they're not from town," Elaine suggested.

When the figure emerged from the car, they could see clearly that it was a man, but in the growing darkness, he was too far away for them to make out his face.

"A man," Jan said. "Do you think it's a romantic rendezvous? Has she been checking the paper all these years to see if he still remembers her? But why now? Why this year?"

"You sound like you're writing the plot of Vanessa van Dyke's next novel," Elaine said.

By now, the man had reached Vanessa, where she still stood in the shelter of the trees on the shore of the lake.

For a long minute, the two of them stood face-to-face. Then they embraced.

"I think it's some kind of romantic meeting," Jan said. "Maybe we should go."

"Um," Elaine said, moving back. "How do we get out of this place? It's darker in here than it was out there."

As she did, she knocked her head against one of the supporting beams of the play structure.

The wood of the ship rang like a hollow bell.

On the edge of the lake, both the man and Vanessa turned toward them. Then the man began to stride toward the landlocked play boat.

"Oh no!" Jan said. She grabbed Elaine's arm and scrambled for the door they'd come in by. "Are you all right?"

"Did they see us?" Elaine asked.

"I don't know!" Jan said as they scuffled out into the relatively brighter twilight.

When they stepped out of the boat, River White stood over them.

"River!" Jan said. "What are you doing here? Did you crack the code in the paper? Are you here to cover the story?"

As the questions tumbled out of Jan and on the other side of her Elaine rubbed her head, Vanessa jogged up.

"What's going on?" she asked. "Jan? Elaine?"

"You know these two?" River asked, with a clear tone of surprise.

"Know them?" Vanessa asked. "They've hosted me at their beautiful house practically every day this week. What are you two doing here? Aren't you supposed to be hosting your private party at the tearoom?"

"What are *you* doing here?" Jan countered. "Are you two an...item?"

River looked at her as if she had grown two heads. "An item?" he echoed. Then he burst out into uproarious laughter.

Even Vanessa looked at them with bemusement. "We've never met before," she said.

"Never met?" Elaine repeated.

"Then why are you here now? Did you follow the code?" Jan asked, looking around. Was it possible that they'd interrupted the wrong meeting? Were the people who designed the code just running late? Or had all this nonsense scared the actual code-makers away?

"The code!" River said, like a scientist shouting *Eureka!* "Is *that* how you two got here? How in the world did you figure out the date?"

"CE," Elaine said simply. "Christmas Eve."

River looked at them with something approaching admiration. "If you two ever get tired of running your tearoom," he said, "I might have a spot for you at the *Courier* as investigative journalists."

"Watch out," Jan said. "I just might take you up on that."

"But why are you here?" Elaine asked. "How do you two know each other?"

"We don't," Vanessa said.

"We just met." River put his arm around her.

"Then how did you know to follow the code?" Jan asked. "And are you the one who put it in the paper?" she asked River, then turned to Vanessa. "Or was it you somehow?"

"No, no," River said. "It was me." He held his hands up as if they had the drop on him. "You were right," he told Jan. "I just couldn't let you know. I was afraid it would mess everything up if anyone found out. And as long as you couldn't figure out the date, I figured nobody could. So our secret was safe."

"I guess we could take that as a compliment if we wanted to," Elaine said.

"Mess up what?" Jan asked.

Vanessa took a deep breath. "I was born in Lancaster."

Jan refrained from telling her that they already knew that. "When did you leave?" she asked.

"When I was just a baby," Vanessa said. "There was a falling out in the family. River's grandmother and my grandmother. They'd always had a tough relationship, but it came to a breaking point, and they made the rest of the family choose sides."

"Our mothers were first cousins," River said. "But they loved each other like sisters."

"Maybe you can understand that," Vanessa said to Jan and Elaine with a smile.

"So they stayed in touch through a code in the paper," River said. "My mother would take out an ad that had a message in it, running down the left margin, about where and when to meet."

"Always at Christmas," Vanessa said. "Both of them moved all over the place, and they didn't stay in regular contact, but his mother would always be there, whenever my mother could get back to town."

"They probably met up a few dozen times over the years," River said. "My mother didn't tell me about it until she was dying, several years ago. She'd been putting those notices in the paper all those years, right under my nose."

"I always knew about it," Vanessa said. "My mother taught me how to check the paper from the time I was a little girl. It might have been the first mystery I ever solved."

"You got the *Penzance Courier*? Even when you moved across the country?" Elaine asked in disbelief.

"The *Courier* delivers to subscribers in dozens of states," River said proudly. "And a number of foreign countries and military bases."

"They'll ship anywhere," Vanessa added. "For a small additional fee. My mother always paid it. And after her death, I couldn't bring myself to cancel the subscription. I just kept reading up on the local news. It got so I started to fall in love with Lancaster."

"And then this year," River said, "I guess I started to get a little—" He paused. "Sentimental. I always knew I had other relatives, ones we hadn't talked to in years. But I didn't know who they were. And I didn't know how to get in touch with them. I actually tried searching for the name Vanessa was given as a young girl..."

"Vanessa van Dyke's a nom de plume," Vanessa admitted.

"But I couldn't find anything," River said. "So I thought, why not put some codes in the paper this year, just like my mom always did? What's the harm?"

"So that's why you went to all the trouble," Jan said. "You couldn't just call, or send an e-mail or a text..."

"Because I didn't know who I was calling," River finished, nodding.

"What an amazing story!" Elaine said.

"I know," Vanessa said. "I feel like it could be a book."

"I can't wait to read it." Jan winked.

"I had no idea I was coming here to meet another writer," River said.

"And I had no idea I was coming to meet an editor." Vanessa smiled at him.

"You know what the crazy thing is?"

"What's that?" Vanessa asked.

"All this time, I actually did have your name and address. In the subscription records of the paper. But I thought you were just another long-distance subscriber."

"Well, next time you can just pick up the phone and call," Vanessa said.

"I'm planning on it," River said. "And in the meantime, I can't wait to introduce you to the rest of the family."

"I hope," Vanessa said, "it's the start of something new for us all."

CHAPTER TWENTY-FOUR

I didn't think that you could make this place any more beautiful," Vanessa breathed. "But look at this! You did!"

Elaine beamed.

Archie had been agitating for several weeks to light every candle in the place at once. As far as Elaine knew, neither she nor Jan had given final permission to his scheme, but in their absence in the last hour before the party, Archie had apparently taken things into his own hands.

Not only were the two parlors spotless, with no trace of the giant rush of clientele the tearoom had served earlier that day, but Rose and Archie had set up the west parlor with piles of food presented between swags of red velvet and scattered with juniper branches. All this was illuminated by an incredible array of candles—candelabra after candelabra, as well as a huge collection of independent candlesticks—in holders of pewter, red glass, silver, hand-turned wood. And every single candle had a warm, flickering, glowing flame.

The effect was spectacular, like wandering into a glen full of captive fireflies.

The Christmas glow was only increased by the swags of holly and mistletoe that Archie must have climbed up on a ladder to weave through the branches of the chandeliers that hung in the dining room and the east parlor.

And in the time since Elaine and Jan had been gone, several of their friends and family had trickled in and were already enjoying their mulled cider and Christmas cookies, ham sandwiches, fresh salad, and, of course, Jan's scones.

Elaine was pleased to see Brody and Sasha, dressed in a beautiful red velvet dress, talking happily with Geraldine, Archie's half sister, who was wearing a satin shirt in a bold green plaid. As Elaine watched, her son, Jared, and his wife, Corrie, walked in, preceded by Lucy and Micah. Elaine hurried over to envelop them all in hugs. As Corrie helped the kids out of their winter coats, Jared made a beeline for his sister, Sasha, giving her a big embrace before he even got his own coat off. Elaine smiled, watching them. Now that they were grown up, it was always a gift to see her kids in the same place at the same time.

"I have to admit," River said, standing nearby, "I thought Candace was a little cracked when she came back to the paper all excited about Christmas at the tearoom in Lancaster. But now," he said, his voice full of wonder, "I see what she means."

"Macy!" Vanessa cried, going over to hug the hotel proprietor, who had a cookie in one hand and a scone in the other.

Whatever else Macy might have to say about the tearoom, Elaine reflected, she was at least enthusiastic in her enjoyment of their victuals.

"Merry Christmas!" Vanessa said, releasing Macy after kissing both her cheeks. Bob had been talking with Macy, but as soon as Jan walked in, Elaine noticed with a smile, he only had eyes for her. He greeted her with a kiss, then stood beside her, his arm around her both protectively and proudly.

Elaine looked around the room, anticipation blending with a little knot of worry in her stomach. Nathan wasn't there yet. Would he be? And what would she say to him if he came?

"And what is this?" Macy asked, spying Jan's ring.

Jan held her hand out, blushing.

"What does it look like?" Bob asked with a wink as Macy grabbed Jan's hand, taking in every detail of the ring.

"You two are tying the knot?" Macy asked.

"Yes, ma'am," Bob said. "Just as soon as I can get this little lady down the aisle."

"That ring is beautiful," she told Jan, who smiled.

"I know what you're thinking," Bob teased Jan. "You're thinking, I should leave this party right now and bake another batch of practice scones."

"Or wedding cookies," Jan told him.

"Or I know what! Why don't you call around a few dozen places to see about a venue for our wedding tea," Bob joked. "I bet you can get in touch with all kinds of people on Christmas Eve."

"You're right." Jan leaned into him. "I should just enjoy the holiday."

"A wedding tea?" Macy asked, looking around at the fabulous setting of the Christmas party. "Why don't you just have it here?" Macy's tone that suggested the lack of initiative on the part of the cousins never ceased to amaze her.

"Maybe we will," Jan told her, and then she thought for a moment. "You know, this whole time I have been wondering if it might be too difficult for us to host, but now I just think it will make me happy. As long as we have caterers," she laughed.

"I agree!" Bob said with a huge smile. "But...didn't we just say we were going to let the wedding details rest for a day?" he asked gently.

"Fair point." Jan smiled, but clearly her wheels were still turning.

"June!" Vanessa called, waving her hand. "June! Come on over!"

Shyly, June joined their circle.

"Now, who is this?" Macy asked.

"Can I tell them?" Vanessa asked.

June nodded.

"This is June Barnhill," Vanessa said. "Author of *The Crooked Lake Mystery*."

Elaine had never seen Macy look so excited. "I *loved* that story!" Macy said. "You're a wonderful writer!"

"Thank you," June acknowledged, her eyes glowing.

Elaine suppressed a smile at the fact that June had no idea what a tough critic Macy was and how much this praise actually meant.

"I'm so glad you came," Vanessa said. "I wanted to let you know that I had a conversation with my agent this morning and I told her that I had just met a very promising young talent. As I count it, if you collect all the episodes that were serialized in *The Crooked Lake Mystery*, you'd just about have a book. And she says she can't wait to read it."

"Really?" June exclaimed. "This is the best Christmas present ever!"

"Well," Vanessa said, "I know you went to some trouble getting Christmas presents for your loved ones this year. So I wanted to see if I could do a little something special for you."

June pounced on Vanessa with another bear hug.

As the tea wound down, friends like River and Vanessa began to trail out, and Archie and Rose said their own farewells.

"This was lovely," Geraldine told Elaine as she and Archie and Archie's wife, Gloria, stood by the door, thoroughly bundled up against the cold. "It felt like a real family Christmas."

"And that's exactly what we were hoping for," Elaine said, giving her a quick kiss on the cheek and a hug before the three went out.

After their departure, there was no one left at the tearoom but family—which was still a wonderful crowd, and a big one, with all the kids and grandkids, along with Bob.

Now the family began to gather in their own clusters. She saw Sasha lead Brody over to talk with Jan's daughter Tara and her boyfriend, Jack, who was trying to figure out where exactly to put the giant cluster of mistletoe he'd shot out of a tree during one of his wilderness jaunts.

"I spotted it in August," he said. "But I waited till now to bring it down. I wanted it to grow as big as it could."

"I've never seen more than a sprig of it before," Sasha said, looking at the bunch in his hands, which was at least four or five times as big as her head.

"I was hoping for a big kiss," Jack said with a wink at Tara.

Jan had marshaled the grandkids as servers, having them rearrange the chairs and tables so that a long single tabletop led down the center of the east parlor, filled with childish abandon by twins Riley and Max with a motley selection of the tearoom's Christmas decorations. Elaine watched Jan's granddaughter Avery collect several of the holly and carnation arrangements that had decorated the individual tables and nest them together into a beautiful new configuration, while her sister, Kelly, scattered Christmas bulbs and evergreen branches in a pattern that seemed at first to be random but turned out to be surprisingly pleasing. After several moments, Elaine could see their dad, Brian, make a move to jump in and organize things, but his wife, Paula, held him gently back so the girls could do it on their own.

When the decorations were complete, though, Brian did put them to work setting the many places at the table, a task they did with élan. Elaine's own grandchildren, Lucy and Micah, had been pressed by Jan into service in the kitchen itself, Micah carrying out big baskets of rolls and Lucy bringing a large salad, and then Kelly and Avery joined in, carrying out steaming plates of potatoes and vegetables.

Jan's daughter Amy, her hand laid gently on the baby bump that would soon become the newest addition to the family, already sat in one of the seats at the table, obviously grateful to be off her feet.

It was such a rare sight to see all the members of both families in one place that it brought a lump to Elaine's throat, but a smile to her lips, as she looked over the happy commotion of the impending Christmas dinner.

Then she felt a tap on her shoulder.

"Hey, stranger," a familiar voice said.

She turned around to see Nathan. Part of her was so glad to see him that she simply wanted to throw her arms around him. But another part of her held back, uncertain and skittish.

"Can I speak with you for a minute?" Nathan asked.

"Um," Elaine said, not sure she wanted to have this conversation, whatever it was, right then. But Nathan already had her by the elbow and was steering her over to the corner of the room, near the beautiful Christmas tree. Archie hadn't lit the candles that festooned the tree, but it was full of glowing electric twinkle lights that filled the corner with warmth.

"Am I glad to see you," Nathan said, giving her a kiss on the cheek. "These last few days have been crazy."

"What have you been—," Elaine began, but Nathan was already pulling something out of his pocket: some kind of small velvet box.

Elaine looked at it as he lifted it toward her, blood pounding in her ears. Was he really about to propose to her, in front of all of these people? Didn't he know her better than that? Could she give him an answer, without having an explanation about who the woman was she had seen him with the past few days? And, most important, how did she feel? Did she want to say no, or yes?

By the time he held the box out to her, she still didn't have answers to even one of these questions.

Nathan smiled and, instinctively, she smiled back. Whatever storms might be happening in her mind, her heart still had a smile for him.

Because she couldn't think of what to say, she accepted the box from him without words.

"Aren't you going to open it?" Nathan asked.

"Oh," Elaine said. She stared down at the black velvet, with the faint glimmers of candle and twinkle light showing on its sheen.

Then she took a deep breath and opened it.

On a field of velvet inside sat a beautiful pin of a peacock set with a tail of emeralds.

"I know it's quite fancy," Nathan said. "Maybe a little fancier than you're used to. But I know you like peacocks. And I thought this one was just so beautiful. Like you."

"It *is* beautiful," Elaine said, her heart warming as the anxiety over a possible ring flowed out of her. "Where did you get it?"

"Ah," Nathan said. "It's a long story. I actually saw it in a shop in Boston a few months ago, but when I went back to get it for you, the store was closed."

"And you didn't just stop there?" Elaine asked, smiling.

"That's just where the story *begins,*" Nathan said. "I couldn't get it out of my head, and I thought if the store closed, maybe the pin had been sold elsewhere. So I called my old friend Esmerelda, who's a dealer in antiques, to see if she could give me a hand."

"Esmerelda?" Elaine queried.

"She's Italian," Nathan said. "Very smart. And a few days later, she called me back and told me she thought she'd found it. But when she brought it up here a few days ago, it wasn't the right pin at all. It was a bird all right, but the tail was all wrong—I don't even know how to explain it," he said. "But it was not the present I'd dreamed of giving you, let me just say that."

"I can't think of anything more perfect than this."

"Well, you can thank Esmerelda," Nathan said. "She told me she could tell I really cared about this woman I was buying the pin for. And she wouldn't give up. Then the next day," he said, "she found it. It had gone up on an auction site when the stop closed. And because she had a connection with that auctioneer, she was able to get permission for me to buy it before the original auction date. So I had to drive down there to get it in order to have it for you in time for Christmas. I know I've been impossible to get in touch with. And I'm afraid I've been short with you on the phone. But I was afraid if I let you ask too many questions, you might figure out that I was taking these unauthorized trips." He grinned. "And if you asked too much about the trips, you might figure out there was something special in the works. You're such a bright woman that it's not easy to surprise you."

"Thank you so much," Elaine said. "What an incredibly thoughtful present. And what a story."

"You're welcome," Nathan said. "You know, the whole process only made me miss you. I never would have canceled our date, except I needed to meet up with Esmerelda to look at the pin. And we've never been anything more than friends, but Esmerelda's very—expressive. It just made me wish I was with you, instead of her."

Now Elaine did hug Nathan. "I love it," she said. "Thank you!"

As his arms wrapped around her, she realized that, amid all the stress and glitter of Christmas, nothing had felt so right all week.

It made her wonder if she might want to stay in his arms forever.

ABOUT THE AUTHOR

Vera Dodge grew up in small towns in the Midwest. She lives and works in Brooklyn.

From the Tea for Two Kitchen

Cranberry Scones with Cinnamon Glaze

2 cups all purpose flour
6 tablespoons unsalted butter, cut in pieces
5 tablespoons sugar
½ teaspoon salt
2/3 cup half and half
½ cup fresh cranberries, cut in half

1 cup confectioner's or powdered sugar
1 teaspoon vanilla
¾ teaspoon cinnamon
1 tablespoon milk

Preheat oven to 425. Mix flour, sugar, baking powder, and salt. Add butter and cut in until crumbly. Stir in 2/3 cup half and half. Add cranberries.

Flour a surface, and knead dough gently no more than ten times. Pat dough out until it is one inch thick, then cut into eight triangular wedges. Bake 13–15 minutes, until golden brown. Cool on wire racks. Glaze when cool.

Glaze: Mix powdered sugar, vanilla, cinnamon, and milk, then drizzle over cooled scones.

Read on for an exciting sneak peek
into the next volume of Tearoom Mysteries!

A Cup of Grace

by Leslie Gould

The lazy snow flurries drifted to the ground outside the window of the upstairs sitting room as Elaine Cook searched Pinterest ideas on her laptop for the tearoom's Valentine's Day Gala. Next to her on the comfy sectional sat Nathan, sorting through a stack of mail, attempting to catch up on his office work.

He was in a busy stretch with his auction business, with several upcoming estate sales and a conference he was scheduled to speak at in Boston soon. He used an antique silver-plated letter opener on the envelopes. Most, after he skimmed each document, went into the paper bag he'd brought along for the recycling.

A gust of January wind shook the windows of Tea for Two, and Elaine stood and pulled the drapes tighter, hoping to block the cold from seeping into the old Victorian house. When she sat back down, she scooted closer to Nathan. He dropped another envelope into the bag at his feet and then put his arm around her, pulling her close, his blue eyes lively.

"A boring task like this"—he nodded toward the bag of junk mail—"is even enjoyable when I'm spending time with you."

Elaine leaned into him, breathing in the scent of his spicy cologne. "I feel the same way," she said, doing her best to be content in the moment. But she couldn't help thinking of her cousin Jan's upcoming wedding just over a month away. And the engagement of her daughter, Sasha. Both reminders that although she'd been dating Nathan Culver for quite some time, he hadn't proposed.

At Christmas, Nathan's odd behavior had made her dread the idea of having to make a snap decision on their future together. But since the misunderstandings had been cleared up, in the past few weeks Elaine had begun to think more and more in terms of Nathan as not just a boyfriend, but a husband.

She felt sure marrying Nathan was in her future, but she longed for him to confirm the idea with a proposal. The sooner the better, as far as she was concerned. Sure, at first she'd had cold feet with Nathan. But it had been a couple of years now. Things had changed. A lot.

Nathan released her and reached for another envelope as she continued scrolling through Valentine's Day ideas. For their tearoom event, they planned to have a high tea with a string quartet playing Victorian music. Elaine wanted everything to be perfect and welcoming and inclusive. She stopped at a photo of tables decorated with old love letters, photos, and Victorian valentines, all under glass. They didn't have glass like this for every table, but it wasn't a bad idea. They wouldn't have to use glass all the time—just having it as an option for special events would be great though. They could avoid worrying about spills and changing the tablecloths in the middle of special occasions such as bridal showers and weddings. She turned toward Nathan and pointed at the old cards. "Do you have any of these?"

He shook his head. "I found some old valentines in an estate sale a few months ago but they all sold."

Perhaps Elaine could find some elsewhere. Love letters too. Maybe people in the community would loan them to Elaine and Jan for the Valentine's Day Gala.

She kept scrolling and then stopped at a photo of heart-shaped scones. She'd have to speak with Jan about that.

They had a few weeks to pull off a fabulous Valentine's Day event. It would be perfect this time—it was their third try to get it right. It wasn't that the two previous times hadn't gone well. It was just that some people, mainly Macy, had after the fact expressed hurt feelings that they'd been excluded. It wasn't entirely true, but Valentine's Day could be difficult for single people, and Elaine truly hoped to do better.

Absentmindedly, she scrolled down to an image of tea sandwiches cut into heart shapes. She'd ask Jan about those too.

She turned her full attention to Nathan. He was right. It was so nice to have an evening together, even though they were both technically working. She hoped their future would be full of such evenings.

She nudged him. "Anything interesting in your mail?"

"No. Mostly junk and a few bills." He tossed another envelope into the recycling bag.

The next piece was a large white envelope with a fancy return address label. He held it up. "I wonder how I missed this." He read the return address. "It's from an attorney in Tampa."

"My," Elaine said. "That sounds important."

Nathan slid his letter opener under the flap and slit open the envelope. "Except I don't know anyone in Tampa." He pulled out a packet of documents and began reading the cover letter.

Elaine turned back to her laptop and Googled *Valentine Tea ideas.*

But she was distracted from clicking on the first entry by Nathan holding his letter in midair. "Wow."

"What is it?"

"I'm mentioned in Berl Newton's will."

"Berl Newton?" The name was familiar but Elaine couldn't place the man.

"He owned the roadside attraction, you know, the World's Largest Snow Globe."

"Oh, of course," Elaine said. It had been years since she'd thought of the place. Back in the day, everyone shortened the name to simply the Snow Globe.

"He and my dad were friends, way back when," Nathan said.

Elaine and Nathan's fathers were friends too, but she didn't think her own father was particularly close to Mr. Newton. She certainly didn't remember him and his family ever coming for dinner or anything, but she did remember her family visiting the World's Largest Snow Globe. "That skating rink was the best," Elaine said.

Nathan nodded. "I remember my dad saying that Berl put a lot of work into that rink. It started as a shallow pond, but he redesigned it into a rink that opened in late October and didn't close until March."

"Wow, that really is a blast from the past," Elaine said. "I have such fond memories of the place."

"Me too." Nathan smiled at her. "I wonder if we ever skated there at the same time."

Elaine laughed. "I'm sure we did on some wild Friday night during junior high."

Nathan nodded and a sweet expression passed over his face. "I wish I could remember it."

"Me too," Elaine responded. She'd known Nathan much of her life. They were friends growing up and then, as they both married other people and lived their lives, didn't have any contact from the time they graduated from high school, except at her father's funeral, until she returned to Lancaster three years ago.

She loved that Nathan and she had shared experiences from the past—even ones in which they couldn't recall all of the details.

She pointed to the document still in his hand. "So why are you mentioned in Mr. Newton's will?"

"You're not going to believe this."

"Try me," she said.

"He left me the old roadside attraction property. And his snow globe collection."

Elaine's eyes grew wide and she pressed her hand against her chest, her fingers splayed. "You're kidding."

"That's what this attorney, a man by the name of"—he read from the bottom of the page—"Andrew Marner, wrote. Apparently he's handling all of Berl Newton's business. He said that Mr. Newton had taken care of nearly every detail of his will, businesses, and finances. Everything was in order. The attorney doesn't expect it will take long to settle the estate."

Elaine caught her breath. "When did Mr. Newton die?"

"Three months ago." He glanced at the date at the top of the letter. "This was sent just before Christmas." He sighed. "Wow, I totally overlooked it."

It wasn't like Nathan to miss an important letter, but she could see how it could happen. He'd been really busy the last few weeks.

"I hope this doesn't sound odd, but why would he leave it to you?" she asked.

"It doesn't sound odd at all." Nathan ran his free hand through his light-brown hair that was touched with hints of gray. "I have no idea." He put the letter beside him and glanced at the next page of the document. "Like I said, he and my dad were good friends. And several years ago, Mr. Newton contacted me about selling his snow globe collection at auction."

"Did you take it on?"

Nathan shook his head. "He found a collector here in Maine to sell it to, so he didn't need me, but then he changed his mind. He said it had too much sentimental value to sell it after all. I didn't actually see the collection, just photos of it, but it appeared to be quite extensive. Probably one of the best collections around, maybe *the* best."

Elaine had always loved snow globes. "What about that huge snow globe he used to have? The outdoor one."

Nathan turned his attention to Elaine. "You wouldn't be referring to the world's largest one, would you?"

Elaine grinned. At one time, the snow globe put Lancaster on the map, even though the roadside attraction was nearly ten miles out of town. "That's exactly which one I mean."

"Well," Nathan answered, "after the new highway bypassed the place, business gradually died down and Mr. Newton finally dismantled it. My dad had told me that he was afraid it could be hazardous to someone who might trespass on the property."

The globe sat on a pedestal with steps leading to the opening. Inside was a bench with pine boughs suspended over the top of it. The floor was painted white, and white confetti floated down from the ceiling.

She remembered going skating at the rink with her parents and brother several times and then sitting in the snow globe. Mr. Newton hired a photographer sometimes and once her dad paid to have a family photo taken. She'd have to ask her mom about what had happened to the picture.

On Monday mornings at school, the kids would talk about skating there over the weekend. It was the place to be, for a time, for the children and the teens of Lancaster. Skating at the Snow Globe, tucked away in the forest, was much better than skating on Chickadee Lake. There wasn't any wind and lights hung over the top of the rink, allowing night skating. It had been a magical place.

She took Nathan's free hand. "Did you go skating there a lot?"

"All the time," Nathan answered. "I didn't have to pay because of Mr. Newton's friendship with my dad. I was quite the skating pro." He grinned. "Nearly as good as Scott Hamilton."

"So you could do jumps? Axels? Doubles? And triples?"

He laughed. "Maybe not quite that good. But I definitely killed it under the disco ball. You should have seen my funky chicken moves."

Now it was Elaine's turn to laugh. "I'd forgotten all about that." The ball had been hung high over the middle of the outdoor rink. It really had been a magical location.

Sadly, by the time she was in junior high, the place started to fall off the map. By high school, it had closed.

And now Nathan was going to inherit it. It seemed unbelievable. Of course, it wouldn't be the same place now that it had been. It was probably just a collection of run-down buildings. "Do you know the history behind it all?" she asked.

"Vaguely. Mr. Newton's dad owned the property and opened it as an auto camp back in the 1920s when cars were first becoming popular, but those Model Ts couldn't travel very far at once. He had a gas station and a garage and fixed a lot of flats, I imagine."

Elaine remembered her mother talking about family trips as a child when they'd get multiple flat tires in a day because of the thin tires and rough roads.

"According to my dad, Berl's father had little cabins for travelers to rent, and he stocked the pond with fish in the spring," Nathan said. "He had fire pits and hiking trails, a destination along the way for travelers. He added a store and a little gift shop too so he was making a profit from taking care of both the cars and the customer."

Elaine slipped her laptop to the side, and turned toward Nathan, tucking one leg up on the sectional. "When was the skating rink and globe added?"

"Oh, Berl added those after his father passed away. The rink first, in the fifties. And then the globe later, probably in the '60s."

It had been the 1970s when Elaine had skated there. "Did you ever hear why he added them?"

"Yeah, he wanted to draw in year-round business." Nathan had a faraway look in his eyes as he remembered the details. "Travelers took their trips in the summer, which brought in plenty of business, but he wanted an attraction in the winter to draw the locals out. That's why he came up with the rink and the snow globe. He sold little snow globes in the gift shop too, which were a big hit. Of course they were cheap, nothing like the ones he collected. He also turned the cabins into rustic European-style cottages."

Elaine remembered those. They had pitched roofs and shake siding. They looked as if they were lifted right out of the Bavarian countryside. There was also a little chapel on the grounds with a double steeple and miniature stained-glass windows. As far as she knew, services were never held in the building, and she guessed that Mr. Newton had built it as a place where his guests could reflect and pray.

Nathan explained, "He was a sort of Renaissance man. He had a degree in engineering, which he definitely put to use around the property. But he made his living, at least most of it, from selling real estate in the area. I think the whole World's Largest Snow Globe project fed his creativity. His goal was to make the place a winter wonderland, with a snow globe theme."

"Well, he certainly succeeded. I can still vividly remember how magical all of it was. It was like a fairy tale come to life." She smiled at the memory. "So did Mr. Newton move to Florida because the business declined?"

"I'm not sure," Nathan replied. "Perhaps he would have anyway. But I do remember his wife died and he felt restless. He was a good businessman and a big dreamer, and I'm guessing he figured he'd have more opportunities in an urban area."

Elaine could see that.

Nathan slipped the document into the envelope. "The will is dated a few months after the last time I spoke with Mr. Newton, so six years ago." He pressed the flap of the envelope down. "I'll call the attorney in the morning and see if there are any more details."

"This is wild," Elaine said and Nathan nodded, clearly stunned and a little confused. "I guess I just wonder why he wouldn't leave the property to a relative."

"I don't know," Nathan said. "He did have a daughter. She was several years older than we are."

Elaine smiled, recalling the girl, although she couldn't remember her name.

"I can't imagine why he didn't leave it to her," Nathan said. "But even more so, I can't fathom why he'd leave it to me."

FROM THE GUIDEPOSTS ARCHIVES

This story, by Anne Goodwin of Beloit, Wisconsin, originally appeared in *Mysterious Ways*.

Cameron, North Carolina, is a small community known for its antiques shops and Southern charm, but the day I visited back in 2009, my greatest discovery was Miss Belle's Tea Room, a rambling Victorian built in the heart of town at the turn of the twentieth century. Everything on the menu was homemade and delicious: corn chowder, tomato pie, curried Rice-a-Roni salad. Best of all was the coconut cream pie.

"You don't share your recipes, do you?" I asked the woman behind the counter.

She hesitated—"Well, they're a secret. . . . "—but after a little cajoling I walked out with recipes for all the specials that day. I started making the dishes at home back in Wisconsin, serving them to friends and family. Once I got them down perfectly, I even experimented a little, adding bratwurst to the corn chowder. But there was no tinkering with everyone's favorite: the coconut cream pie. It always got rave reviews, usually followed by a request for "the secret recipe."

I don't know how many pies I made over the next few years. They were the perfect way to say thank-you to folks or just enjoy after dinner. I never claimed the recipe as my own, but I didn't go out of my way to reveal where I'd picked it up either. A few years ago, I heard the sad news that Miss Belle's had closed. Did that mean I was the last person still serving her menu?

Nobody got more pies than the staff at my parents' retirement community in Southern Pines, North Carolina, about 15 miles from Cameron. Nurses, administrators, medical aides. Everyone got a slice when I visited. My mother endured Parkinson's and was on a skilled nursing floor. Sometimes I gave out whole pies to thank her caregivers for going above and beyond. I just had to be careful about bringing pie for Mom's fellow residents. I couldn't run afoul of anyone's dietary restrictions.

There was one woman I thought could use a treat. A new arrival to Mom's floor, who was struggling with dementia. She was having trouble adjusting to life in the community and often became confused, upset, or scared. One time I was walking through the common room on my way to the exit when she suddenly appeared at my elbow. "Please take me home," she pleaded. "I don't want to be here. Take me home!"

A nurse gently led her away. "I'm sorry," she told me. "You're not the first one Isabelle has begged to take her home."

Yet, on my following visit, I was surprised to hear the most beautiful music drifting from the dining room, and even more surprised to see who was behind it. Isabelle? She sat at the piano, playing hymns and folk classics. Her songs were like slices of my pie, a little treat to brighten everyone's day.

I was still thinking about Isabelle a week later while I chatted with the staff at the nurse's station. "Anne, you make the best coconut cream pie I've ever had," one of the nurses said. "What's your secret?"

"Wish I could take full credit," I said. "I first tasted that pie at Miss Belle's Tea Room. Sad to say it's closed now, but it used to be in Cameron."

"Cameron, North Carolina?" one of the nurses said. "You know who used to be the mayor of Cameron? Isabelle."

"Isabelle who plays the piano?" I decided then and there to bake Isabelle a coconut cream pie. As mayor, surely she'd visited Miss Belle's. Maybe she even knew the restaurant owner.

The next day I invited Isabelle to my mom's room. I cut her a slice of pie, put it on a paper plate and handed it over. Isabelle studied the pie for a moment and smiled. I held my breath as she took her first bite. Her eyes lit up.

"Now that's *reeeeal* good," she said in a low Southern drawl. It reminded her of her own secret recipe for coconut cream pie, at a place she used to run in Cameron, back when she wasn't discharging her part-time duties as mayor.

It was the best review "my" pie could ever get. From Miss Belle herself.

A NOTE FROM THE EDITORS

We hope you enjoyed Tearoom Mysteries, published by the Books and Inspirational Media Division of Guideposts, a nonprofit organization that touches millions of lives every day through products and services that inspire, encourage, help you grow in your faith, and celebrate God's love.

Thank you for making a difference with your purchase of this book, which helps fund our many outreach programs to military personnel, prisons, hospitals, nursing homes, and educational institutions.

We also create many useful and uplifting online resources. Visit Guideposts.org to read true stories of hope and inspiration, access OurPrayer network, sign up for free newsletters, download free e-books, join our Facebook community, and follow our stimulating blogs.

To learn about other Guideposts publications, including the best-selling devotional *Daily Guideposts*, go to Guideposts.org/Shop, call (800) 932-2145, or write to Guideposts, PO Box 5815, Harlan, Iowa 51593.

Sign up for the Guideposts Fiction Newsletter

and stay up-to-date on the books you love!

You'll get sneak peeks of new releases, recommendations from other Guideposts readers, and special offers just for you . . .

and it's FREE!

Just go to Guideposts.org/Newsletters today to sign up.

Guideposts®

Visit Guideposts.org/Shop or call (800) 932-2145

Find more inspiring fiction in these best-loved Guideposts series!

Mysteries of Martha's Vineyard

Come to the shores of this quaint and historic island and dig in to a cozy mystery. When a recent widow inherits a lighthouse just off the coast of Massachusetts, she finds exciting adventures, new friends, and renewed hope.

Tearoom Mysteries

Mix one stately Victorian home, a charming lakeside town in Maine, and two adventurous cousins with a passion for tea and hospitality. Add a large scoop of intriguing mystery and sprinkle generously with faith, family, and friends, and you have the recipe for Tearoom Mysteries.

Sugarcreek Amish Mysteries

Be intrigued by the suspense and joyful "aha!" moments in these delightful stories. Each book in the series brings together two women of vastly different backgrounds and traditions, who realize there's much more to the "simple life" than meets the eye.

Mysteries of Silver Peak

Escape to the historic mining town of Silver Peak, Colorado, and discover how one woman's love of antiques helps her solve mysteries buried deep in the town's checkered past.

Patchwork Mysteries

Discover that life's little mysteries often have a common thread in a series where every novel contains an intriguing whodunit centered around a quilt located in a beautiful New England town.

To learn more about these books, visit Guideposts.org/Shop